# THE *Magical* MERMAID *and the* MOON

# THE *Magical* MERMAID *and the* MOON

*A Fairy Tale about How the Tides and Waves Began*

## Angiah Harris

Indigo River Publishing

**Indigo River Publishing**
3 West Garden Street, Ste. 352
Pensacola, FL 32502
www.indigoriverpublishing.com

Editors: Hannah Fortna and Regina Cornell
Book Design: mycustombookcover.com

Ordering Information:
Quantity sales: Special discounts are available on quantity purchases by corporations,
associations, and others. For details, contact the publisher at the address above.

Orders by U.S. trade bookstores and wholesalers: Please contact the publisher at the
address above.

Printed in the United States of America

Library of Congress Control Number: 2019937650
ISBN: 978-1-948080-89-7

First Edition

With Indigo River Publishing, you can always expect great books, strong voices, and
meaningful messages. Most importantly, you'll always find . . . *words worth reading.*

*This is dedicated to those of you that have loved and supported me unconditionally. I thank you from the bottom of my heart for helping me navigate the waves of life. You are loved.*

# Prologue

**At one time in Earth's magical existence, beautiful, mystical creatures existed alongside human men and women.** These creatures were just as domesticated as any human today and inhabited all parts of the world, including the entire body of water that makes up Earth—the ocean. During this time, the ocean didn't experience tides and waves. The waters were still. Not even the strongest of winds could move them.

On land lived creatures, such as early humans and other animals, that walked on two legs, lived off the land, and respected one another, just as the world works today. In the water, the ways of living were similar to life on land for the laughing dolphins, singing fish, dancing turtles, and many other creatures that lived in the enormous sea. They had families who loved and fought together, rules and basic laws that kept everyone feeling safe and secure, schools that taught ways of life, and jobs that helped support the societies. The undersea creatures worked hard to promote peace among themselves and for the most part enjoyed their beautiful lives together.

Of course, there were also creatures who did not fit into that peaceful lifestyle. Many of these creatures were outcasts, hating the world they lived in, looking for any reason to be negative. When enough of them got together, they called themselves a "mobile kingdom," because they stuck together at all times and were family to one another. A mobile kingdom never settled down in one place. They were always on the move, only stopping to rest and regroup for a few days at a time. When they stopped, they ravished the land and stole from the creatures who lived nearby. The peace-loving creatures of the world knew to avoid the mobile kingdoms at all costs.

Within the ocean's perfectly calm water stood the largest kingdom of all the kingdoms. Known as the center of the world, it was home to thousands and thousands of creatures who loved to sing. Yes—sing! In the distant past, singing was a powerful thing, and it helped spread peace and love throughout the land and sea. The underwater kingdom was full of creatures old and young, big and small, with different voices, who took to the streets each day singing and playing with one another. These creatures sang about everything—from how delicious their dinners had been the night before to the loves of their lives. They sang their inner songs and expressed their feelings in each moment. Ringing with singing voices, this wonderful kingdom lit up the sea with its vibrant colors and a positive energy that couldn't be matched by any other place in the world.

The kingdom was governed by a mermaid king and mermaid queen who were full of love and life. Every chance the couple had, they went out into the streets with their people to share food, sing songs, and enjoy one another's company. The mermaid queen's beauty was hypnotizing— long golden hair, hazel eyes, and pure, clear skin. She was very smart, with a beautiful way with words, and she found many solutions to the problems that arose in the kingdom.

Her husband, the mermaid king, was considered a god for his breathtaking appearance. He had polished silver hair that shone brightly whether it was day or night, the physical strength of at least a thousand men, and flawless skin despite the many battles he'd been in when he was younger. The mermaid king loved to sing and spent many of his days singing with others and enjoying life. His voice was said to be magic—he could cure the worst sickness and defeat an enemy in the same breath. Because of this, he was known as a "song wizard" across the many kingdoms. Indeed, his bloodline was thought to be the last of such wizards, who could alter appearances, manipulate objects, and even hypnotically influence others with their powerful voices. The mermaid king chose to use his gift for good and would only use the magic when it was needed most. He believed everyone had magic within, so he lived his life without judging others, always remaining open to every possibility, and tried to inspire his subjects to be fully themselves because only then would their real magic come out.

The king and queen loved their people and were willing to do anything to keep them happy and loving life. The royal couple had a daughter, the mermaid princess, whom they loved more than anything in the world, and for her sake as well as for the sake of their people, they worked hard to foster and maintain peace. Under their rule, their kingdom became one of the most prosperous kingdoms in history.

# Chapter 1

# The Valley of Stones

**The stillness was almost suffocating as the general made his way through the vast, unfamiliar darkness.** He, more than anyone besides the king himself, should know all the water territory, how far it reached, and how deep it went—yet here he was, uncertain and slightly anxious as to what he would find.

Even he, the great general of the mermaid king's army, feared the unknown.

However, his thirst for his dream outweighed the fear. So he inched forward.

The dark, still water seemed to grow blacker the farther he traveled. Hesitating for a moment, the general began to rethink his plan. Should he change his mind, plan something new? Then he noticed, off in the distance, a dim light shining through the black. He blinked. Was his mind playing tricks on him?

But no—the glimmer was still there! Relief flooded his body. It had to be what he was searching for. He began moving again, picking up his pace, drawing nearer and nearer to the light until he finally stood before it—exactly what he'd hoped to find.

The glimmer of the rock was intoxicating. He'd heard the myths of the valley in which he now stood, that hundreds of thousands of earth stones and crystals were buried deep beneath millions of tons of water in the earth's crust. The stones in this particular valley were said to drain any energy source of its life force if the creature vibrated at a certain rate—the vibration that could be attained by singing or creating music of any kind. These stones' primary purpose was to turn the stolen life force into amplified energy and return it to the earth to keep the planet balanced. Some people were afraid of the stones and their power. Others believed the earth knew what it needed to do to care for itself and that the stones were simply part of its self-preservation.

In the darkness of the valley, the general remained hypnotized by the stones' thrum. Their energy, unlike anything he'd ever felt, pulsated through his body. He breathed in the stones' power, and as he did, his hatred raged in his heart. Something in the stones' energy pulled at him, connected with him. He and they had been destined to meet and intertwine. He didn't know how or what would happen next, but he was determined not to stop until he'd reached his goal. He whistled into the valley, and when its walls lit up with deadly but beautiful crystal stones bulging out of the earth's crust, he knew he now had what he needed—his weapon. Now he could set his plan in action and fight to become what he believed himself destined to be.

A king.

# Chapter 2

# The Mermaid Princess

**The mermaid princess knew she was venturing farther than she ever had.**

It was a sunny day, the sunlight filtering down through the water, warming everything in its path and glowing in the princess's beautiful purple hair and stunning eyes, which everyone said reminded them of perfect mornings when the sun was just rising. The ocean was as calm as ever, and as the princess traveled, she sang about the beauty around her, about love and life—the things she'd been taught to love by her parents, the kingdom's beloved king and queen, and to sing about so that her love would spread to those around her. Like her father, the princess often sang and danced with the people in the kingdom, and she knew by the smiles on their faces, even the people who had almost lost their will to sing, that she made a difference for them.

Many even said the princess's voice was more magical than her father's.

On this beautiful day, as the princess sang, she continued to travel farther and farther from the kingdom. As she'd grown older, her love for exploring the vast waters had increased, and though she always tried to remain mindful of where she was so she would hear her father singing for her to come home at the end of the day, she loved going on adventures and seeing new things, meeting different creatures, learning about where they lived, and experiencing the connection she realized all creatures in the world shared—the ability to create art and song.

But today, she sang distractedly—she was still thinking about what had happened the day before and had been thinking about it almost all night.

There was something dark about the outskirts of her father's kingdom. The farther she went from the kingdom's center, the more creatures she met who seemed sad and despairing, and the dimmer and less vibrant the plant life became. Yesterday, she'd asked her parents about the sadness and where it came from. Her father had answered with such conviction, she could swear the whole castle had shaken with each word: "There are so many creatures in this world, some are bound to be sad, angry, and hateful, and it's because of this darkness that we can know the light—true happiness, true beauty, true strength. But I don't think the sad creatures are destined to be lost in the dark, and that's why we sing to them. We try to sing them into the light, although sometimes they choose to stay in the dark. And though we don't know why those creatures ended up in the darkness or why they choose to stay there, it's certainly no coincidence that we find them and sing to them. If, even for an instant, they see any glimpse of light because of our singing, we've helped them more than we can even understand. I hope, my child, that you never fall into the pit of sadness, anger, or hurt—because it's a dark place where anyone can end up, even you—but if you do, remember that no matter how dark it may seem, light travels at amazing speeds and always finds a way to shine through."

And last night, still thinking over her father's words, the princess had decided to do something she'd never done: travel beyond the outskirts of the kingdom, even farther into the darkness, to discover what caused it.

*If I find what makes the darkness*, she thought for the twentieth time, *my father can put a stop to it.*

She was now well beyond the kingdom's limits, much farther than she'd ever been before. The farther she swam, the darker the world became. Plant life was scarce, and there were no other creatures nearby.

*Strange*, thought the princess. *I thought the sea was full of life everywhere.*

Suddenly she noticed a distinct change in her surroundings—the water was darker and colder, and the sunlight was dimmer, more eerie. Glancing upward, she realized some sort of haze in the water was blocking out the sun's warm rays. The cold seeped into her skin, turning into fear when it reached her heart.

*Maybe I should turn back.*

She was just about to turn around when something caught her eye—some sort of light in the distance through the haze. Squinting, she looked harder, but she still couldn't tell what it was.

She needed to move closer.

Below her, old structures—once parts of old, forgotten kingdoms or large objects dropped from above by land people—cluttered the ocean floor. Suddenly apprehensive, she thought that if she swam in the shadows of these structures rather than out in the open, maybe no one would see her. Swimming under the unrecognizable ruins, near the sandy ocean floor, she moved closer to the mysterious light.

The nearer she drew to the light, the brighter the surrounding water became. Soon, the broken structures began to take new shapes.

*I think this is some sort of city*, the princess thought.

She was sure of it when she realized she wasn't alone— other creatures were swimming near her, heading the same direction, toward the light, as if they were gathering for a town meeting. She could tell at a glance that they were different from her father's subjects in the kingdom. Something about them made her want to hide even farther in the shadows. They were all dressed like soldiers, in dark camouflage colors, an extreme contrast to her own brightly colored clothing. For a moment, she paused to catch her breath, hiding from sight in the shadow of a rock and listening to her heart pounding like thunder in her ears.

*No one's singing*, she thought, suddenly realizing that she'd stopped singing too. *Where am I? Who are these people?*

No one seemed to see her. They kept moving quickly and quietly toward the eerie light.

*Maybe I've gone far enough.* She could turn around now, go back to the castle, and tell her father what she'd seen. Then he could bring his soldiers here, beyond the kingdom's limits, to investigate this strange, frightening place.

Suddenly, she heard a loud, booming voice from the direction of the light. A voice she thought she recognized.

*It couldn't be—could it?*

She had to find out for sure. Creeping forward from shadow to shadow, she followed the dark people as they moved toward the light and the voice. Moments later, she realized she'd reached the town center, where all the creatures had gathered around an enormous rock—a crystal of some sort, the princess assumed—foggy white and shining bright like the sun itself.

The crowd seemed to be looking at something or someone in front of the massive crystal. Still keeping to the shadows, the princess maneuvered herself to gain a better view. She tried to hear what the people near her were whispering, but she only caught a word here and there—she thought they were talking about their leader, about an event that was about to happen.

*Where are we?* the princess asked herself again. Had she wandered into a neighboring kingdom? Why was it so dark here, and why was everyone dressed like a soldier? Was this one of the mobile kingdoms her father had told her about? With thoughts racing through her mind, she carefully moved closer to the crowd.

All at once, the clustered people hushed. The shouting voice spoke again.

"Gather, my comrades—the time is upon us to make our war and strip the mermaid kingdom of its king!"

The princess's heart stopped as the crowd suddenly cheered. She *had* recognized the voice.

It was the shark general, her father's best friend.

# Chapter 3

# The Reveal

"My comrades, we are here today to discuss war and new ways of life in the sea."

The shark general's voice was almost hypnotizing. The glow from the large crystal behind him highlighted his body, muscular and suave, and his big teeth and dark eyes. It also reflected off his clothing—the traditional uniform of the princess's kingdom—and glinted on the gold mingled into the fabric. The gold that labeled him a member of the royal household. Gold, the element that was said to be so powerful it should only be trusted to those leading nations to peace. Yet here he was, her father's best friend, a creature she'd come to know very well and even love, standing before her, speaking treason to a large group of oddly dressed creatures in the middle of nowhere in the deep sea.

The princess felt paralyzed as he continued speaking.

"For too long we have been oppressed and made to live in a world that we do not love! A ridiculous world—a careless world. All that excruciating singing all the time, always playing and laughing! Well, the time has come, my comrades, for us to take over and remove that so-called god of a king! I have just what we need to overcome him and his magic and wipe him off the face of this planet!"

The crowd erupted into cheers as the shark general raised his hands and motioned to the large glowing rock. As he continued speaking, the princess listened in horror, so distraught she barely heard his words as he ranted about how terrible the kingdom was and how there would soon be a time when singing was outlawed. Tears welled in her eyes as each word spoken by this all-too-familiar voice and each cheer from the crowd drove the betrayal deeper into her heart. She thought of her father, her mother, and many other creatures of the kingdom. Their hearts would break when they found out about this.

The shark general's speech ended, and someone else took over. The crowd was now riled up even more, and the princess couldn't bear to hear what else they had to say. She closed her eyes, desperately gathering her thoughts, slowly breathing in and out, and trying not to panic. For the first time in her life, she felt intense fear clutch her heart.

*How could the shark general do this to us?* she thought. The world seemed to be slipping out from beneath her, but she knew she wasn't safe in this foreign place. She needed to leave as quickly and quietly as possible to get back to her father and report what she'd just seen and heard. Breathing in and out deeply one more time, she turned to leave.

"Why, Princess—my eyes did not deceive me! What are you doing here, so far away from your precious kingdom?"

The princess froze, paralyzed by fear. Then she turned slowly.

The shark general and two of his men stood before her. The men were sharks, just like the general, with big shiny teeth and what appeared to be very dark eyes. They were dressed in dark, camouflaged military clothing that was decorated with medals as if they were highly ranked. The creature to the left of the shark general stared at the princess as though he wanted to rip her apart. The other shark appeared to be second in command. The princess noticed his eyes were more gray than black; somehow this made them seem less intense than the other soldier's.

"It's a shame you had to be here today to hear our plan." The shark general's voice was firm. "You were supposed to be home when I took your father out and killed him—to fall into my arms for consolation. You, and your mother, who, in time, would have become my wife. But how can this happen now that you've heard our plans?"

The princess's blood boiled at these words. This creature in front of her had watched her grow her whole life and witnessed her mother and father's beautiful marriage.

She knew her mother would never agree to what the shark general suggested. Gathering her strength, she forced the words from her mouth. "She would never marry you. You will not get away with this. My father is the most powerful song wizard in the ocean, and with just one song, he will strip you and all these fools of your lies, deceit, hate, and—"

"No!" The general cut her off. "No, he will not. The time has come for darkness to rise and for your idiot father and all his light and singing to fall. I have a weapon so powerful not even his silly little fight song will matter—a weapon strong enough to wipe out singing completely."

As he spoke, he reached for something in his breast pocket and pulled it out. The princess had never seen such an object before. It appeared to be another stone or a crystal of some sort, similar to the glowing rock at the front of the town center but molded into a wand shape. The shark general held it up, and at that moment, as the other two sharks followed his gaze, staring up at the elongated crystal, the princess made a break for it.

She swam only a short distance before she was wrestled down and detained.

*Song,* she thought desperately. *I will sing a song—then someone will come to help me!*

She opened her mouth to sing, but one of the soldiers pressed a gag into her mouth.

Her father's enemy laughed. "Foolish girl—you do not believe me! But know that you have now made my job easier.

Tonight, I will trick your father into coming to find you, and we will search for you together. He won't know what's coming. Then, you will see my true power and understand why you will never sing again. Soon, *I* will be king!" He turned to his gray-eyed second-in-command. "Take her away, to somewhere no one can find her or hear her in case she decides to sing."

The princess struggled and screamed through her gag all the way through the town. Then the guards took her through a series of underground passages, so she knew no one saw where she was being taken. Momentarily, she would make eye contact with the gray-eyed guard, but his partner quickly pushed her forward each time.

They continued for quite some time before they reached a holding cell of some sort, into which the guards placed her. After they left her alone, the princess screamed for help and even tried to sing, but she heard no response. There was nothing recognizable in sight, and the still waters seemed darker and quieter than she'd ever seen them. Exhausted from screaming, the princess finally sank to the ground next to the door, crying. Would her father be able to save her? Would anyone?

# Chapter 4

# Fun and Trickery

The mermaid king and queen were out in the streets with their people, singing, eating, dancing, playing, and preparing for the festival planned for later that day.

"Will our lovely daughter be joining us today, or has she run off to explore the world?" the queen asked her husband as she prepared some of the dishes for the feast.

The king moved around the table, examining the different fruits and vegetables, and laughed. "I saw her scurry off earlier, so I don't think we will be seeing her until dinnertime."

The queen giggled, then said seriously, "Do you think it's okay that we let her go off and explore alone? She's such a curious girl, and curiosity can get you into trouble. I don't want our daughter lost in the world out there."

The silver-haired mermaid king stared at his beautiful bride in her golden blouse as she spoke. Her hair shone in the sun, and a dimple appeared in her left cheek when she smiled. He loved everything about her—how she worried about things he never even thought about, how wonderful a mother she was to their beautiful child—and he was grateful to call her his wife. She was his soul mate, and he couldn't imagine life without her by his side.

"My love, don't worry—our daughter is very special indeed. The light that radiates from her inner being will always triumph over anything and will always keep her safe. One day, she will rule this kingdom, and all her travels will make her that much more of a successful leader. Do not worry—light will always be on our side." The dashing king swept his wife into his arms and kissed her gently on the forehead. Then he moved his lips to her ear and whispered, "I love you."

The queen rested her head on his chest and wrapped her arms around him, feeling the air become electric, as it always did when they were together. She whispered, "I love you too."

Soon, creatures from all over the kingdom arrived and began to feast. Everyone laughed and joked while eating together as a community. Elders told stories of the past as children ran around playing tag and hide-and-seek.

The day crept into the evening, and the mermaid king noticed his daughter was still absent from the gathering. He began to ask her friends if they had seen her. None of them had. Neither had any of the townspeople with whom she typically spent long amounts of time talking or singing. The king found this odd. He decided to go to the top of their castle and sing his daughter's favorite song that she liked to hear at the end of the day to pull her back home. She'd once told the mermaid king that the song made her feel as though she could never be lost in the sea, because no matter where she was, his voice and that song would always guide her home. He noticed his wife engaged with a group of creatures, so he quietly slipped away and made his way to the family castle.

The castle was gigantic, and its every wall was beautifully colored. Because the castle had been built by the mermaid king's ancestors, each of whom were members of the wizard bloodline, each brick in the castle's walls glowed in the dark with magic. Windows everywhere let the sun into more rooms than the king and his wife and daughter needed. Often, friends and those who needed somewhere to sleep lived with them in the castle. The king felt it was important to be kind to others even if they could never repay the kindness, so if someone needed a hot meal or a warm bed at night, the palace doors were always open.

The silver-haired king finally arrived at the highest balcony in their home, with a clear view down to the streets and all throughout the kingdom. He loved being up there and seeing everything below. It reminded him that everyone is a small part of a much bigger picture.

With love in his heart, he began to sing. "My child, my heart, where could you be? Come home, and tell me all your adventure stories." His voice rang out, and those below cheered and sang too. The king heard his queen's voice joining in singing with the crowd. He continued on with his song till it was finished, then waited anxiously to hear his daughter's angelic voice sing back to him above the cheers of the excited crowd.

But he didn't hear her.

Suddenly, he saw movement below—someone or something was moving quickly toward the crowd. Was it the princess? It seemed unlikely—she'd never done such a thing before. Feeling uneasy, the king quickly left the castle to confront whatever was approaching them.

"*Halt!*" the mermaid king screamed at the moving blur.

Whatever it was came to a screeching halt, kicking up ocean sand and blocking the king's view. "My king!" the familiar voice said from the sand cloud. "The princess is in danger. I was too late—they took her!"

The sand settled, revealing the king's best friend and right-hand man, the shark general. He spoke in broken sentences, catching his breath. "He told me—I tried to find her—I was too late."

"Silence!" roared the king to everyone in sight. The crowd stopped its chatter instantly. "What is this you speak of? Gather yourself and inform me, brother!"

The shark general slowed his breath and regained his composure. "I was out doing my afternoon swim around the kingdom earlier today when a creature flagged me down in the outskirts. Regular townsman—I sensed nothing suspicious about him—so I approached him and listened to what he had to say. He said he'd seen the princess go exploring today and that maybe I should go make sure she was all right. He mentioned that today's energy felt especially heavy and that he wasn't sure what sorts of creatures would be out. I thanked the creature and headed in the direction he said he'd last seen the princess going. I swam farther and farther, and it seemed like the water grew so much colder. It's not like it used to be out there, brother—we have much we need to explore."

The crowd gathered closer as he spoke.

"I swam forever and almost gave up, thinking she might have headed back—but then I heard a scream! I moved as fast as I could in that direction. I was surrounded by strange, dark creatures that didn't notice me. And then I saw. My king, the princess was being roped down and taken prisoner." Everyone gasped. "I wanted more than anything to save her, but I was outnumbered and might have lost both of our lives in the process. I turned around and came straight here, my king!"

The king stood frozen like a statue, absorbing everything the shark general told him. The crowd was silent, and his queen was watching him, but he couldn't find words to speak.

"This is *war*!" blurted the shark general.

"No," the mermaid king said calmly.

The queen stepped forward. "We are a peaceful people. A war is not the answer."

"She's right," said the king. "We are a peaceful people. But—" Anger chased the feeling of surprise from his mind.

"This gesture is a declaration against *me* and *my queen*. These people dare take our daughter, the final remaining member of the song wizard bloodline of many generations of mermaids, and use her as bait. Bait for a *war*! Well, they will get their war, but not the one they're expecting. It has been a long time since I've used my magic for anything other than love, but today I will unleash a fight song like no other before, and they will feel my wrath!"

"I will assemble the troops!" said the queen.

"No," the king said before she could move. "I will go, and I will go alone! I will face these creatures who have taken our daughter, and I will return home with our child. When we return, we will celebrate our victory. Do not worry, my love!"

# Chapter 5

# The Death of Song

**The mischievous shark general was burning on the inside with glee as he listened to the mermaid king and queen.** The leaders of the kingdom were experiencing a moment of strain, and he knew it was because of him.

He had waited a long time for this moment.

The shark had come to the kingdom as a young boy, separated from his family, who had been lost to one of the largest storms of the century—although it still hadn't been strong enough to move the calm ocean waters. He'd been found days after the storm by the mermaid king's mother, who was the queen at the time, as she was out with rescue teams helping manage the aftermath. He'd hit his head in the storm and was still unconscious when the queen found him, so she took him back to the kingdom to care for him until someone came looking for him. Once he came to, he couldn't remember his family or where he was from. Word was sent out, and they waited for his family to return, but they never did. The queen took the shark in as her own and raised him next to the mermaid king as his brother, and as they grew up together, the mermaid prince became more powerful as a song wizard, and the shark grew in combat skills and physical prowess.

Then the young mermaid prince had made a simple choice—a choice that had sparked the rage and hatred in the shark general's heart and continued to fuel his vengeful plan as he rose through the ranks over the years and eventually became general to the king. The shark general knew the king had always appreciated his loyalty, but the mermaid would soon learn that his loyalty had only ever been a disguise for his hatred.

Trying to hide his excitement about how well his plan was working, the shark general shouted, "I will lead the way to where I saw them, my king, and I will fight by your side!"

"Thank you, brother. Let's go!" The king and his shark general set off into the night.

***

They'd been swimming for hours when they began to notice, off in the distance, a dim light.

"There—let's move," said the king.

But before he could continue forward, the general said, "No, let me go. You stay back, and I will go see what's going on. We can't risk your being captured. I'll see if there are any traps or anything to be concerned about."

The mermaid king reluctantly agreed and watched as the general headed toward the dim light in the distance. Much time passed. The king grew anxious waiting for his general to return, but still he did not. Something clearly was not right.

*I have waited long enough*, the king decided. He followed the general's trail with urgency, kicking up a cloud of sand behind him. Before he'd gone far, he rounded a corner, and the sight beyond was so surprising he stopped dead in his tracks.

A large gathering of creatures he didn't recognize stood facing him like statues, staring at him with their dark, judging, hateful eyes. The mermaid king was taken aback.

He slowly searched the crowd with his gaze for the shark general or the princess, but he did not see them. After moments of silently surveying his surroundings, the king yelled, "Who is in charge here?" His voice was so strong it shook the entire crowd.

Silence followed. The creatures continued to stare at him with a darkness in their eyes.

The mermaid king continued. "I am searching for my daughter—she was taken. My general and I are out looking for her. We mean no harm; we just need your help in finding her."

Still, no one responded.

Then something began to happen. The crowd parted, making a pathway for the king. He hesitated, confused by the silence, but decided to make his way through the crowd to whatever or whomever they were parting for. He moved slowly past the creatures, searching their eyes for a glimpse of life. He could now see their camouflaged clothing, and he realized they were all dressed the same. Everything and everyone was so dark and uninviting. He searched the creature's faces, looking for a sign that someone would help him, but he found only darkness. He was alone. Where was his general? What had happened to the shark? The king was surrounded by the enemy with no one to help him.

But still he was unafraid.

Moments later, the mermaid king reached the center of the crowd—and what he found sent a rage surging through him like he had never felt before.

Here stood the shark general, holding his daughter in chains.

The king's eyes moved back and forth from the shark general to the princess. His heart pounded a thunderous roar in his chest, as if it were trying to escape from his body. Every part of the king wanted to tear the shark general apart. He tried to move, but the sight of his brother holding his daughter in chains and the thousands of dark eyes surrounding him paralyzed him.

The shark general let out a howling laugh and began to speak. "The king is here. The king is here," he mocked.

"He has finally graced us with his presence." The shark laughed again. "Oh, Princess, you should feel honored that your father ventured out by himself to find you. It made my job that much easier. I surely thought we would have to fight a few of your so-called soldiers."

The king stood shocked and silent, listening to his supposed friend speak so proudly to him and the crowd.

"Tonight is the night that everything changes," the general continued. "Tonight is the night that darkness prevails."

"What is the meaning of this?" screamed the mermaid king, finally finding his voice. "How could you do this, my brother, after everything we've been through?! My mother was your mother, my daughter your daughter, my kingdom your kingdom!"

"*No!*" said the shark general. "Your mother was your mother; she took pity on me, but you were the apple of her eye. She did not care to hear me sing; she only wanted to hear you. She did not pay attention to or praise the things I did for her. And the kingdom—it was always yours. I've hated you and your kingdom my whole life. I was never one of you. And now I've built my own kingdom with others who feel the same as I do. It has been our vow to each other that one day we would find a way to silence your and the kingdom's songs, and that day has come!"

\*\*\*

The princess stared into her father's eyes, terrified. She wanted desperately to scream to him about the stones, but she'd been bound and gagged again earlier by the gray-eyed guard and another soldier. She'd thought, surely, the first face she'd see coming through the doors would be her father's, not a guard's. But then she'd been dragged out here to wait among these dark creatures, and the general had appeared beside her. "Your father is here, and you will watch us kill him," he'd told her.

Now, her father stood before her, and she could see the shock on his face as he listened to the shark general's mocking. Her heart broke for her father, and she wanted desperately to break free from her chains and run into his arms.

\*\*\*

The king spoke, sincerity deepening his voice. "I'm very sorry you and all of these creatures feel that way. We have never forced our way of life on anyone; you are all welcome to live how you feel suits your needs. Release my daughter so we can leave this dark kingdom you have created. We will never return. We will leave you and your people alone and live peacefully next to each other in the sea."

The shark general laughed cruelly. "This is not an option, my king. We do not want to share the sea with you anymore, and we will not. I said it in so many words earlier, but let me say it again: this is *war*. We are prepared to battle your fight songs and end your reign as king and the reign of singing."

The general's words shocked and angered the mermaid king. He looked again at his daughter in chains, and a storm brewed inside him—a fight-song storm.

He had used fight songs in the past to defend the kingdom from attacks after his parents died, when he became the king. Typically, his men would engage in hand-to-hand combat alongside him to fight off enemies. Many of the king's enemies believed they had a chance against his soldiers, but as soon as the mermaid king began to sing the fight songs, the enemy stopped in their tracks, broken down by the melody and tune of his magical voice. By the time the song was finished, the fight was long gone and the enemy soldiers had either fled or found themselves at peace, their negative energies healed by the vibrations of the king's songs.

Perhaps the same thing would happen to this crowd of enemies.

"Very well," shouted the king. "If it is a fight song you all want, that is exactly what you will get!"

\*\*\*

The princess struggled to break loose from the chains. With her mouth gagged, she tried to scream "no!" to her father and gesture toward the stones, but she knew she was powerless.

She would have to watch.

Her whole heart hoped the stones would be no match for her father's voice, but something inside her knew otherwise. She watched as her father rose in the air above the crowd, expanding his chest, preparing to sing. She shook her head over and over as much as she could, but her father, not understanding her, just looked at her with a calmness in his eyes. His beautiful silver hair was glowing more than she'd ever seen before, and his royal golden sash shone brightly.

With love pouring out from his face, he stared at her and began to sing.

The tunes and melody started low and began to increase, gaining momentum. The energy around the princess and the crowd began to circle and sway to the melody of the mermaid king's voice. The words escaped his lips and expanded into a ball of visual energy near him. For a brief moment, the princess thought maybe he would win—but then she noticed something terribly wrong.

The energy was not expanding outward through the crowd as it should. It was expanding above her father, as if it were restricted and attached to just him. The princess looked at the creatures in the crowd around her. They all held crystals, pointing them in the direction of her father.

And next to her, the shark general held the biggest crystal of all.

The shark general laughed again and shouted to be heard over the king's song. "Do you feel your power draining from you, sire? Do you feel everything for which you exist being erased? That feeling is these powerful crystals sucking your energy from your being. We found these crystals across the world, in the deepest and darkest depths of the ocean, where all you could see were the stones in the night."

The mermaid king continued to sing, but an energy field surrounding him trapped his words and their energy, containing his fight song and turning it inward on himself, ripping his body apart.

The shark general raised his voice again. "The natives living where we found the stones said the stones have the power to strip a creature of all of its energy if harnessed correctly. It took me years, but I finally figured out how to wield the stones, to harness the energy, and to destroy what I hate most—the light created by song!"

The princess kept her eyes on her father, who was growing weak. Hatred rose in her for the shark general and his arrogance.

"One night," the shark general continued, "I was out attempting to activate the stones when I heard a few creatures off in the distance singing. The stones began to vibrate and glow as I moved closer to the group of singing dolphins, and suddenly I realized the dolphins were growing weaker—as you are now—as the stone came nearer to them. Their songs faded, and the stone grew brighter. I tossed the stone beneath them and watched a ball of energy form around them. They didn't realize what was happening, and suddenly they exploded into a ball of light, which entered my stone. Then I knew the power I'd found—the tool to kill song itself."

The king continued to sing, forcing the words from his mouth, but the stones pulled the energy behind his words into themselves, draining the mermaid king. His vibrance was fading away.

The princess fought again, trying to break free, but she couldn't move as she watched her father's life force flow out of him. Seconds later, the king fell silent and dropped to the floor. The energy around him formed into a large sphere as the stones continued to vibrate and shine brightly. The king looked at his daughter.

"I love you, my dear," he said. "Please have no fear; light always finds a way. It is always near."

A bright light exploded. The princess closed her eyes against the brightness, and when she opened them again, the king was gone.

The stones lit up, and the crowd let out a loud, violent cheer.

The princess's body began to shake violently. She

felt as if her heart had been ripped out of her chest, and she couldn't control the violent tremors. Then her head struck a nearby rock, and the world went black.

## Chapter 6

# Alone

**Time blurred.** Had the princess been imprisoned for a week? A month?

She was kept alone in a faraway prison, moved to the remote spot shortly after her father's death so that, she assumed, she wouldn't break free and escape to the kingdom to tell her mother what had happened.

But though she was far from it, she knew the kingdom was in ruins.

At the moment of her father's death, an electromagnetic pulse had spread throughout the entire ocean, killing much of the beautiful plant life and the sea's vibrance. The shark general and his men had then invaded the happy kingdom and wiped it clean of all remaining colors and singing. When the guards had moved her to the new prison, the princess had overheard them speaking. They said her mother was being held a prisoner in their dungeon because she refused to become the shark general's wife. The princess knew her mother was far too smart to believe any lies he told her about what had happened.

The guards had also said that only they and the shark general knew the princess was alive and where she was—the rest of the kingdom, including the shark general's army, thought she was dead. The princess hoped her mother did not believe this lie, but as time continued to tick away, she feared her mother would have no other choice.

The princess learned quickly that no one could hear her in her prison. She'd tried screaming at the top of her lungs, but no one ever came to rescue her, and her surroundings remained quiet. She never heard a passing creature or even saw a flying bird passing over her prison. Everything was dark. Only the dim sun, hiding behind the clouds in the day sky, and occasionally the stars at night provided any light.

In her prison, the princess was supplied with a certain amount of food. She saw the same guards only when they resupplied her stock, which seemed to be frequently—their way of spying on her, she assumed. She was surprised that the general fed her, but then she overheard one of the guards saying the shark general hoped keeping her alive would one day play in his favor. She had no idea what that meant.

Other than the guards' visits, she remained alone.

The prison was a large enclosure. The princess had plenty of room to swim, and because the prison's walls extended above the water's surface, she could look out above the water but couldn't see over the walls, out to the rest of the sea and land. She imagined the prison looked from the outside like the top of an open volcano rising out of the ocean. It was as if the walls touched the sky.

Though she'd been in and out of consciousness on the way to the prison, she remembered quite a bit of travel, so she knew she was in an uninhabited part of the sea. An enormous rock in the enclosure—she imagined it had been placed there by giants—gave her a place on which to sit and stare at the sky. The princess hadn't sung since watching her father die, although sometimes she felt the urge. She would stare at the stars at night, admiring their beauty and thinking that they were the only light left in the world when they managed to peek through the heavy clouds. They gave her the smallest amount of hope and comfort.

The general could not destroy the stars.

After months of solitude aside from the guards' brief food deliveries, one afternoon, the shark general finally visited the princess.

She hadn't seen him since the night he'd murdered her father.

He was dressed differently but still in royal clothing—dark fabric, darker than she'd ever seen, with the royal gold embedded into it. He had a stunning ruggedness that even the princess could not ignore, but her hatred for him easily overshadowed this.

The general smiled at the princess as he entered the enclosure. "How are you enjoying your stay?" he said smugly.

The princess sat in silence as she watched him move around her enclosure.

"Do you have enough food?" he asked. "Is there something you need?"

Silence smothered the space between them. The shark general glanced around the princess's new home, but she could tell he was keeping his real attention focused on her. Why was he looking at her that way? She knew her flowing purple hair had grown out more since he'd last seen her, and streaks of beautiful silver were emerging in it; was he admiring her beauty? She kept her pale eyes glued to him, staring almost through him, as he made his way around her space.

The princess gritted her teeth but chose to respond carefully and quietly. It took every ounce of her energy to not attack the shark general.

"You have taken everything from me," she said calmly and firmly. "You will never have anything I need. The minute you killed my father, you killed something inside of me that will never be revived. Your day will come when you pay for what you've done. So unless you want to set me free and return my kingdom to me, I never want to see your face again!"

The shark general laughed. "As stubborn as your father, I see. I wish you were more like your mother. She is starting to come around to our new way of life, and if she knows what's right for her, she'll agree to be my queen!"

"She will *never* be with you!" the princess shouted. "She will *never* love you the way she loved my father—and neither will I!"

The shark general laughed again. "We will see, my dear princess—we will see. I hope one day you learn to live with the darkness. Otherwise, you will die here alone."

The princess stared at the shark general, contemplating attacking him, but she knew she would never overpower him. She slowly turned her back to him and said, "Then I choose to die alone." She waited for him to leave.

"What a waste!" the shark general spat as he slammed the door closed behind him. He locked it and disappeared from sight.

# Chapter 7

# A Magical Introduction

The princess felt pain in her chest with each beat of her heart, and tears began to roll down her cheeks as a sadness she hadn't felt before swept over her.

She felt defeated.

*Mother thinks I'm dead, my father is dead, and the kingdom I call home is no more*, she thought. *What is the point of living anymore?*

The day was shifting to evening, and the princess floated over to the giant boulder in her enclosure and propped herself up on it.

*The stars—all I have are the stars.*

She replayed the shark general's visit in her mind—the way he moved, the hurtful sting of each of his words. She wondered why he was the way he was, battling with her conflicted feelings. She had loved the shark general as she would love any family member. If he hadn't been the one who betrayed the family, he was right—she would have gone to him for comfort. She wondered if her mother felt like she did, alone, with no light in the world. She felt sadness for her mother and what she'd experienced—losing the two loves of her life in one moment.

The princess was also sad for the whole kingdom. She loved her people but could not protect them from this. Guilt settled over her as she watched the daylight fade away.

Then, to her surprise, thousands of stars emerged in the night sky—a beautiful sight for the first time in many months. She stared in awe, and the sadness and despair that had swept over her gave way to a sweeping hope.

And she began to sing.

As the melody picked up, the words poured from the depths of her soul. She sang, and tears poured down her cheeks, but instead of feeling drained, she began to feel energized. Something was different—she could feel the light inside her soul burning brightly. She finished the song but continued humming the tune, smiling.

Then something began to happen in the sky.

The bright stars drew together into a circle of light above her head. She decided to dance. As she spun in circles, her speed increased and energy built around her and then burst, sweeping over her, engulfing her in a blanket of warmth. She fell back in delight with her eyes closed.

When she finally opened her eyes, she stared in

amazement—a pure, beautiful sliver of white light had appeared above her in the sky. Bewildered, she caught her breath, afraid it would vanish if she breathed too loudly. She'd never seen anything like it before—it looked like the tip of her fingernail lighting up the night sky. Had she brought this new sight about?

The mermaid princess searched the rest of her narrow view of the sky for other lights like this one, but there were none. She watched it for what felt like an eternity, waiting for something to happen. Then, feeling empowered by the new light's beauty, she decided to speak to it.

"Hello there, you enchanting sight in the night sky. I have never seen you before. Where did you come from? You don't know how happy I am to see you and the light you release. The world is a dark one now, and your light is needed." The princess paused and listened again for anything or anyone, but there was still only silence.

Millions of thoughts crossed her mind as she stared at the new light in the sky. Other people besides her had probably noticed this new sight by now, and she assumed the shark general would immediately suspect she'd caused it and return to her enclosure for another visit. But she was far out in the middle of nowhere, so she knew it would take someone a while to get there, if anyone was coming.

But she still heard no one approaching.

Peace and quiet engulfed the night around her, so she continued speaking quietly and gently about the pain she was experiencing. She spilled her heart to this new light in the sky, and as the last words escaped her lips and the tears gushed down her cheeks, she exhaled. She hadn't realized it, but as she exhaled, it felt as if she were releasing a breath she'd been holding since the moment her father died. As she'd spoken to the night sky, weight had lifted from her with each word that had left her mouth. She stared at the sliver of light and felt herself begin to relax for the first time in a while.

A gentle breeze pushed through her enclosure, causing a whistling noise. The breeze was nice on her skin, and she liked feeling it flow through her beautiful purple hair. She lay there, eyes on the evening sky, enjoying the moment, until she fell asleep.

A while later, the princess woke to the sound of a strong wind. Looking up, she realized the new sliver of light in the night sky had sunk nearer to the horizon. She sat quietly, listening to the wind around her, and suddenly, she thought she heard a faint whisper. She froze. Was someone nearby, speaking? She listened harder. What was the whisper saying?

The wind picked up, and the voice grew louder and clearer. As she listened, she gradually made out the words: "It is all right, my dear; I am here now."

*Who is here?!* she thought.

Confused, she glanced around, but she saw no one and nothing except the sliver in the sky, which appeared to be shining brighter than before.

The whisper continued. "Please do not be afraid. I awoke here in this new place—the vibration of your tears and pain and of the love behind your singing caused me to illuminate. I have been observing. I am sad to see this is not a happy world currently, my dear, and I am sorry to have found you like this. But do not fear; all will be set right in this world—it always is."

Suddenly, the princess realized the whisper was coming from the sliver of light in the sky. She felt paralyzed with confusion. What was happening? Was her father speaking to her through the light? Was she dreaming?

Just then, a strong gust of wind pushed past her, and the voice spoke again. "I am the light you see in the sky, and I am happy to have found you, my dear."

Overwhelmed with emotion, the princess smiled uncontrollably, and the sliver in the night sky shined even brighter than before.

"That is what your people need from you, my dear," the light's voice continued. "They need that smile and your love."

The princess's smile faded. "They all believe I'm dead, along with my father. How could I ever give them what they need from here? I am a prisoner."

The princess heard a slight chuckle. "You are no prisoner, my dear," said the voice. "Yes, you are currently physically confined, but the only prison that exists is the one in which you keep your heart. All situations are temporary, and they are what you make of them. I am so very sorry you are confined and that the world you experienced with your father is gone, but it is not dead, my dear. It is only dead if we give up. You cannot control this confinement, but you can control how you treat yourself in it. Do not give up on light and love. You have a gift, my dear—I can feel it vibrating off of you. You have just lost sight. Do not give up or give in. I will help you remember; I will help you find it again."

The princess, somehow no longer upset, found comfort in these words. Something deep inside her knew the voice spoke the truth. "Okay," she whispered. "How will you help me, my new friend? What do we do?"

"Do not worry—the solution will present itself," said the sliver in the sky. "All we can do right now is just be."

The princess realized the night was ending and that her new friend was disappearing as daylight approached. "Will you be back tomorrow?" she asked.

The wind, now calmed, faded along with the gentle whisper. "I cannot promise this, my dear—no one can guarantee returning tomorrow. But I will tell you this: I am very real in this moment, and so is the universe, and we have always been here and always will be. So even if I do not return one day, know that I am alive and shining bright for those who have lost their way in the dark. You have now seen my light with your own eyes and heard my voice with your own ears. Light always finds a way."

And then the breeze ceased, and the sliver dipped below the horizon.

The princess could hardly believe what had just happened. She felt more alive than she had in some time.

*Light always finds a way*, she repeated over and over in her head. She'd heard her father say this many times throughout her life, and now her new friend had repeated it. It was truth! As she watched the sunrise behind a patch of clouds making their way across the sky, she felt tired again, as if she hadn't slept in the many months she'd been a prisoner there. She eased herself into her hard bed and drifted away, thinking of her conversation with the light in the night sky.

# Chapter 8

# Orders

In the palace of the murdered mermaid king, the shark general, who had proclaimed himself the shark king, wrapped himself in his golden royal attire, which revealed his arms and many scars.

His third-in-command stood before him to deliver a status report. "Sir, we have rounded up all rebels and properly disposed of them. There should be no more singing protests in the square—we made good examples of those creatures."

The shark king gazed down at the shorter soldier. "Good job, soldier. Keep an eye out for anything suspicious, and continue to make sure all residents understand the new laws."

"Yes, sir!" barked the third-in-command.

It had been many months since the shark general had betrayed his closest friend, killed him, imprisoned his daughter and wife, and taken over the kingdom to become the new king. Now, standing here in the palace he'd claimed for his own, he thought back to what had happened after he'd killed the king—when he'd returned to the kingdom without the mermaid king or the princess and had explained to the queen that her husband had been defeated attempting to save their daughter, who had also lost her life, from the mobile kingdom that had captured her. He'd explained that he'd battled alongside the king but had escaped, covered with nearly fatal wounds, which he'd secretly inflicted himself, when he realized it was hopeless.

He remembered the queen's despair at his words, how quickly she'd spiraled into depression, and how this had allowed the general to bring his soldiers into the city over the next few weeks without her noticing. The kingdom had grown darker and darker, and finally the general had launched his full takeover of the city. The queen had remained confined to her room until she emerged, furious, to confront the general about what one of her servants had just secretly reported to her—that the general was taking over the city, stripping homes of color and forcing the citizens to wear crystals that killed them if they sang; that large numbers of creatures who resisted the nonsinging rules were disappearing; and worst of all, that the shark general had said the changes had been ordered by the queen herself, rendered hopeless by the death of her husband and daughter.

The general had denied nothing. He spoke of the new kingdom, persisting in his claim that he'd had nothing to do with her husband's and daughter's deaths but was simply taking the king's place, renovating the kingdom to suit his style. He invited the queen to rule by his side. When she refused, he threw her into the dungeon, officially claimed the role of king, and passed the title of general to his second-in-command.

"Sir, another matter needs to be discussed." The third-in-command's voice brought the shark king back from his memories.

"What?" the new king barked.

"The new light in the sky at night. There's a lot of chatter around here as to what it is. Do you think the princess has something to do with it? Should we be concerned?"

The shark king visualized the light sliver in his mind and remembered when he'd first seen it, traveling home from his only visit to the princess. He wouldn't dare tell the soldier how he'd truly felt the moment that sliver of light appeared in the sky—how for the first time since beginning his reign of destruction, he'd felt fear. Refocusing his attention on the soldier, he said, "I am not worried about this light. I just saw the princess, and she is defeated and broken—this is not her work. We will issue an announcement that the light is something we're tinkering with, so no one tries to rebel any more than they already have. Then, we will wait and see what, if anything, this light in the sky will do."

The soldier nodded once.

"Send our new general to the prison to check on the princess," the shark king continued, "and have him set up camp near the prison for a few days to see if anything out of the ordinary occurs. When I receive his report back, we will reconvene to discuss whether anything needs to be done."

"Aye, aye, sir." The soldier exited the room in a hurry.

The shark king, now alone in the room, stared at the book-filled walls. He'd been spending more and more time in the library and had converted it into a meeting room where his top soldiers could present reports to him. It was the only room he'd kept the same in the castle, though he'd destroyed much of the rest of the interior, and he made sure his soldiers and his council knew it was off limits, his own sanctuary—just as it had been when he was a boy. He remembered sitting in this room when he was young, reading, imagining a different life, one where he was happy. When they were children, the mermaid king had always been singing throughout the hallways, while he had locked himself in the library to read a good book and try to drown out all the noise. Unlike the mermaid king, the shark had never been happy—could not remember a moment in which he'd felt happiness. So far, ruling this kingdom made him feel the closest to happy he'd been, but he still felt a huge heaviness on his heart and had no idea how to remove it.

He thought again of the sliver of white light in the sky. Had he ever heard or read anything about such a thing? He could not recall ever hearing of it before. Of course, everyone knew of the sun and the stars, but this thing seemed completely new. Whenever his eyes looked upon the sliver in the night sky, he felt a sense of fate—a sort of dire connection—in his heart that he could never reveal to anyone. He hoped it wouldn't interrupt his plans to rule, that the crystals would continue to work in his favor and give him everything he ever wanted.

He couldn't worry about his apprehension of the new light. Now, he needed to make sure the princess was checked on again and the public service announcement was issued to ease the people's fear. Then he could wait for answers about this new mystery in the evening sky.

*Chapter 9*

# The Gray-Eyed General

**The third-in-command soldier entered the chamber of the gray-eyed shark, the new general of the shark king's army.**

The gray-eyed shark's study was dark and simple, lit by two low candles and a white crystal in the corner of the room. He had no need for many possessions, so his room was almost completely empty besides the bed he slept on and the chair he read in. Aside from the few books lying around, there was little evidence he was staying in the suite.

When the third-in-command arrived, the gray-eyed shark had just stepped back inside from his patio, where he spent many of his evenings staring out above the kingdom. He was unused to the attention he received now that he was in charge of the army, especially after feeling invisible most of his life. He wasn't sure he liked it. In the dark, he'd felt like he fit in, but now he stood out more than he would have ever expected. He'd accepted the promotion to the role of general with no hesitation. He'd do anything for the shark king, even if meant being uncomfortable. The shark king had rescued him when he was an orphaned teenager, after he'd been beaten, robbed, and left for dead by members of a mobile kingdom, and then he'd cared for him, raised him, and trained him as a warrior, so the gray-eyed shark owed the shark king his life. But now, because he was still accustomed to isolation, instead of diving into the community, the new general had begun delegating more and more of the public work to the third-in-command.

The soldier who now stood before him.

"Sir," the soldier said, "the king has requested that you take a trip out to the princess to make sure she is not the one behind the light in the night sky. He would also like you to camp out for a week or so, watch for anything suspicious, and then report back."

The gray-eyed shark adjusted his new royal clothing, which didn't quite fit his strong, solid body. "Would he like to meet with me before I go?" he asked.

"He did not say, but it seemed he does not," said the soldier. "Would you like me to go ask him, sir?"

"No. I'll go and return with my report in a week and a half."

"Okay, sir—I will let the king know," the third-in-command replied. "Remember your stone, my friend—it is your only defense if she sings."

The soldier left the room.

As he prepared to leave, the gray-eyed general laughed to himself at the third-in-command's final comment.

*Defense against what?* he thought. *What—will she kill me by singing? I watched her father die, and he was more powerful than she is.*

He had heard rumors of healing properties and magic in her voice, but he hadn't witnessed such things, so he didn't believe it. Neither did the sliver of light that had appeared in the sky bother the gray-eyed shark, but he was curious to see if it was indeed the princess's magic.

Despite his beliefs that she was no more powerful than anyone else, he found himself thinking of the princess often. Something about her had struck a chord in him, and he often volunteered to take the princess her monthly supplies, using the task as an excuse to be near her. He remembered how he'd felt when they dragged her limp body out of the city after they had murdered her father. As he'd watched her slip in and out of consciousness, he'd felt something—but he couldn't figure out what it was.

Even the shark king didn't know this, but the gray-eyed shark had seen the princess for the first time long ago, when he was a teenager, long before she became a prisoner under his watch. One evening, after his training with the shark general, the gray-eyed shark teen, frustrated that he lived alone beyond the kingdom's limits while the shark general lived within it, had decided to secretly follow the shark general back to the outskirts of the then-colorful kingdom, just to see what it was like. As he approached the kingdom, he noticed that the colors and the sound of singing and laughter increased the closer he got to the city. Suddenly, the gray-eyed teen, still hiding in the shadows, saw someone or something hurrying toward the shark general. At first the teen couldn't make out what it was, but he quickly realized it was a beautiful mermaid, around the same age as himself, with vibrant purple hair. He moved closer for a better view, and he heard the mermaid calling the shark general Uncle and him calling her princess—it was the daughter of the mermaid king, whom the shark general had conditioned the gray-eyed teen to hate. The mermaid hugged the shark general, the gray-eyed teen's savior, and he cringed at the sight of it. Then he watched them both swim toward the singing and the light together.

After that, filled with curiosity he couldn't ignore, the young shark teen had begun to follow the shark general regularly and watch him from afar. One afternoon, while following him, the gray-eyed teen became distracted, lost sight of the shark general, and found himself in a different area. As he started to panic, fearing he would run into old enemies, or anyone at all, he suddenly heard singing. He hid. Moments later, the mermaid princess came swimming by, singing a tune. He watched her glide by gracefully and listened to her soft voice. She swam leisurely, as though she had nowhere especially to be, and he assumed she would just pass by, but then she stopped and began exploring the area. His mind raced. Did she know he was there? What would he do if she found him? He watched her from the shadows as she reached for a flower on the ground and picked it up—then suddenly he realized she'd seen him. His heart dropped, and he held his breath as she stared past the flower, directly at him. She opened her mouth as if to speak, and he darted off. Fearful she'd tell someone she'd seen him, he never ventured near the kingdom again after that.

He hadn't seen the princess again until they'd found her spying on the town meeting.

Suddenly, he found himself envisioning her light-colored eyes, and he snapped himself out of the thought. He had a job to do, a king to serve, and he had to travel quickly. He finished gathering his needed supplies and hurried off toward the prison.

*Chapter 10*

# A Lost History

**The mermaid queen sat alone in the palace dungeon, which had become her home when she refused to rule the kingdom next to the new shark king.**

Because the shark king feared that if any other prisoners were near the queen, she would lead them to mutiny, he moved them to other places and ordered the guards not to engage directly with her. When they entered her cell with her food rations, she had to turn her back to the entrance and drop to the ground with her hands behind her head. At first, the mermaid queen resisted, but after numerous scuffles, she finally became compliant with this rule, realizing it was not the time to fight.

Before now, she'd never paid attention to the dungeon of their castle, and now she wondered if her late husband had known of the terrible conditions their captives had lived in all those years. They had left the law enforcement and anything related to war to the shark general, as he was much better suited for it.

As she sat alone in the dungeon, the queen continued to replay her last moments with her husband in her head, watching him swim away, never to return. She had known something had happened, and her fears had been confirmed when the shark general came stumbling back into the kingdom without her family.

She still didn't know whether the shark general was responsible for their deaths or if his seemingly newfound thirst for power had simply grown with her husband gone.

***

In the months that had passed, she'd learned very little. She wondered how many of her people were still fighting the darkness, but she could hear nothing beyond her cell and learned nothing new from the guards who fed her. The shark king visited her, attempting to explain his love for her and how the new way of life could be just as good as the previous, but she would say little, making sure he understood she would never stand by his side in darkness.

She could never truly tell him how it hurt her deep down inside to deny him.

Despite his darkness, which she could never support,

she loved the shark king. When she looked at him, she didn't see the cold new king that everyone else saw; she only saw the young shark who had adored her since the moment they'd met many, many years ago.

The queen had always known that the shark had liked her from the moment they'd locked eyes in child-hood. At that time, the young shark had been excelling in combat school and rising through the ranks alongside the young mermaid prince, who was learning to use his wizard power correctly and to be a proper king. The young mermaid queen had grown up actively participating in her community. She liked to help plant gardens and had joined outreach groups trying to bridge the gap between the mobile kingdoms and the community. As she'd grown up beside the mermaid prince and the young shark, she'd been smitten with them both but found herself drawn to the shark boy that the prince's mother had adopted and raised as her own. The queen had noticed he was always reading—when he wasn't working hard to rise through the ranks in combat school—and that he was very quiet but also direct and charming when she spoke to him one on one. She knew that the shark felt he could be himself with her—that she saw into the void inside him but didn't run the other way. They would stay up late watching the stars, sometimes talking, sometimes just lying quietly.

The queen knew the young shark had fallen in love with her.

One day, when the shark was in the city, the silver-haired mermaid prince, clearly unaware of the special time spent between the shark general and the queen, had asked the young queen to go on a date with him. She accepted the invitation. Only when the shark returned from the city did the queen learn that he had planned a beautiful evening for them both and wanted to ask her to be his. But it was too late—she liked the mermaid prince and had been delighted when he'd asked her to go on a date. And the shark general would never have another chance after that, because the queen fell deeply in love with the mermaid prince and eventually became his queen. Although the shark never showed it, the queen knew deep down that she had shattered his heart into a million pieces.

And now, the shark had played a role in her husband's death and was asking for her hand. What could she possibly do?

As she stared blankly at the torn-apart walls surrounding her in her cell, she hoped for a solution. She could not give up hope. She had to remain strong.

# Chapter 11

# Awake and Confused

**The gray-eyed shark found himself approaching the prison much sooner than he'd expected.** He'd barely stopped to rest—he assumed the shark king would want to know his report on the princess as soon as possible, so the sooner he could get there, the better.

As he neared the hidden enclosure, the sun dipped beneath the horizon, changing the sky from a brief canvas of colors to almost black. As the light faded, the gray-eyed shark wondered if anyone had stumbled across the enclosure, which he realized stuck out like a sore thumb with its walls that reached to the sky. He quietly and quickly swept through the enclosure's surroundings, searching for any signs of life or disturbance, but because it was harder to see without the sun, he decided to set up his camp. He would continue to survey the area when the daylight returned.

But first, he thought it would be the ideal time to spy on the princess, since the new light had not yet appeared in the night sky.

*We'll see if she summons this light in the sky*, he thought as he approached the enclosure. *We'll see just how powerful she is.*

The gray-eyed shark found the princess not moving, appearing lifeless in her enclosure. Was this why the new light had not yet appeared—because the princess was unable to summon it? He cautiously inserted the rusty key into the keyhole and turned it slowly, then paused. Surely she would hear him. But she remained still, so he entered quietly.

Inside the enclosure, he moved toward her still body with a silent urgency. Paranoid thoughts crossed his mind.

*This is a trick; don't fall for it. She's going to spring up and try to escape.*

He was almost to her when he noticed her subtle breathing and realized she was asleep, not dead or plotting to attack him. He relaxed a bit. As she slept, he watched her, staring at the curves of her lips, the shapes of her closed eyes, the way they moved beneath her eyelids. Her beautiful purple hair lay perfectly on her head, just as vibrant as it had been the first moment he saw her as a young shark. She hadn't changed much with age, but he felt he had. Glancing down at his scar-covered arm, he snapped himself out of his thoughts.

He began to search her enclosure for anything odd, keeping his eyes locked on the princess every chance he got. She continued to sleep, not moving at all, despite any noise the gray-eyed general made. After finding nothing but the crates of food and supplies he himself had delivered, he decided to swim to the surface and look around.

He examined the enormous boulder bulging out of the water and found the area where he could tell the princess sat and stared at the stars. He pulled himself up, keeping his lower half in the water, and propped himself against the rock to look around. He glanced upward and stared in surprise—the half sphere of light, no longer just a sliver, had appeared directly above in the sky.

He dropped into the water and looked down toward the princess. She remained in the same position and had clearly done nothing to make the light appear. Confused and curious, the shark moved back above the surface, again face to face with the light. He examined it with his gray eyes and watched it as it lit up the sky. The stars around it shone as well, and the gray-eyed general realized that he had not actually stopped to look up at the sky like this for a very long time. As it had been all that week, the wind was blowing strongly. The shark listened to it whistle around the walls and up into the air, toward the light in the sky.

*I should go now*, he thought, and he pulled himself away from the breathtaking sight. She would probably wake up soon, and he didn't want to be caught.

After taking one last long look at the sleeping princess, he exited the enclosure and headed back to his camp. He needed to rest so he could rise early the next morning to do his surveillance. In his camp, he lay there, staring up through the still waters toward the light in the sky, thinking of the beautiful sleeping princess, until he drifted off to sleep.

The next day, after sleeping much longer than he expected, the gray-eyed shark general examined the rest of the area and found no signs of any other creatures or disturbances. He decided to return to the enclosure—the princess was probably awake now, wasn't she?

When he arrived at the enclosure, he found the princess awake and eating a carrot fruit. His heart raced when he saw her conscious and moving around. She hadn't seen him the evening before, and he wouldn't let her now.

*I will watch and report back*, he told himself. *That's all.*

# Chapter 12

# Another Reveal

**The princess slowly opened her eyes, feeling refreshed.**
Several days and nights had passed since her first encounter with the sliver of white light in the night sky. She'd slept a deep sleep almost the entire time since then, making up for all of her lost rest. Each night, the white light grew in size; now, it was no longer shaped like a fingernail.

Glancing around, the princess tried to guess the time of day and determine whether anything had changed. She watched her chest rise and fall with each breath as she reflected on her conversation with the mystical light in the night sky. She could hear the whistling in her ears and feel the warmth in her heart. Something shifted within her, and she knew she could no longer sit around and wait for something outside of herself to save the day.

She rose from her bed and stretched her arms above her head, deciding she would find something to eat. Glancing around at the food crates, she realized there was enough food to feed a whole village there. She rummaged through a box, and when she found her favorite carrot fruit, she quickly bit into it. The juices exploded against her taste buds, shooting a positive chemical reaction down her spine that sent a tingling feeling throughout her whole body. It was the first time she could actually taste anything since her father's passing.

As she ate, the princess glanced around the prison enclosure, seeing it almost through different eyes. Until now, she hadn't realized how the depression had closed her eyes to the world around her, but now she noticed the many useful tools among the array of items that had accumulated over the months in her enclosure. Continuing to eat and humming a tune, she started to sort through the items, and she quickly realized she would be able to create a type of paint. She loved to paint—it reminded her of the beauty of the world. She believed that all creatures in the world should be able to mix together beautifully as the paint on her canvas did.

Finishing the last of the fruit, she set to work creating the paint.

***

The gray-eyed general watched the princess through cracks and crevices in the enclosure. He felt a low vibration in the air, and the crystal around his neck occasionally flickered as he moved around.

The princess was creating beautiful colors from random supplies around her, and the gray-eyed shark was intrigued by this glimpse of her creativity. As he watched, she began to dance and throw the new colors at the wall, slowly creating a masterpiece. She laughed, humming louder as she threw different colors every which way, as if in a trance.

Finally, she screeched to a halt and stared at the piece, as though she was fighting to catch her breath. The shark's breath had also sped up, and he tried to slow his as well. He stared at what she had just created. Even from where he stood in his hiding place, he could tell the piece was marvelous.

***

The princess was happy with her creation; there had been no colors like these since the death of her father, and she found them refreshing.

She wanted to share what she'd done with her new friend in the sky.

She tossed aside her supplies, raced to the surface, and propped herself up on the rock to greet her new friend, who had already appeared.

"Hello!" the princess called. "I am so happy to see you again, my friend. You're even bigger and brighter than before!"

The wind picked up and wrapped around her, as if to embrace her.

"I painted today, and I have to say, seeing the colors made me feel more alive. I'm not sure what I'm going to do to help the world, but I have to do something."

She sat there in silence, waiting for a response. She heard no voice, but as the wind continued to wrap around her, she heard a magical humming. As she looked up at the bright light in the sky, now so much larger than it had been, she smiled.

*\*\**

The gray-eyed general decided to enter the enclosure after the princess disappeared above the surface.

Inside the enclosure, he positioned himself behind the supplies to get a better view of what the princess was doing. From his hiding place, he examined what she had just created on the wall. It was beautiful—a collage of colors that seemed to change into different images when he looked at it from different angles. He'd never seen such a sight in such a dark place.

What was she doing up on that rock of hers? He knew he needed to stay quiet and out of her sight, but he had to find out what was going on. As far as he could tell, she was just sitting on the rock, maybe singing. He wished he could hear her. Then he remembered his mission: he had to discover whether she *did* have something to do with the light.

Near the top of the giant rock that rose all the way to the surface, the shark noticed a part of the rock that he could swim up to and underneath without being detected. It was close enough to the princess that he'd be able to see and hear anything he needed to, so he made his way to it and settled himself in the hiding place. He could now hear the princess near him; she was speaking out loud to the light in the sky.

She spoke about her mother and father and of different adventures they'd had as she'd grown older. The gray-eyed shark general found himself hypnotized by the princess's stories, and he longed to look into her eyes as she told them. The wind blew hard all around them as she spoke, entrancing him even more, and his crystal quietly vibrated underneath his royal clothing, responding to some unknown cause. After listening for a while, the gray-eyed shark decided to leave before the princess noticed him.

*The princess isn't doing anything wrong here*, he thought as he headed back to his camp. *Who is really the threat?*

His mind wandered.

***

The mermaid princess felt relief after blurting out her stories and memories for what felt like hours. She listened to the wind slam into the walls of her enclosure, not caring that her friend wasn't talking, although she hoped desperately it would. She needed to find a way to defeat the shark king. Could the light in the sky give her that answer?

She sat in silence, deciding how to bring up the question. Should she not even ask? But finally she gained the courage.

"What do I do, my light friend? I'm desperate for answers. Our kingdom cannot live in darkness for the rest of our days."

Her pulse beat fast, and she felt her cheeks flush. A strong gust blew in, and on it came words.

"Be patient, my dear—the day will come. I feel your energy, and I feel the energy needed to defeat the darkness growing. That is why I grow in light. Be naturally you, despite the current circumstances, and the right things will come of it. Thank you for sharing the things in your heart with me tonight. They were beautiful."

The gust of wind blew out just as fast as it had blown in. Confused by the advice, the princess just smiled and lay in silence. What had the light meant with those words? Despite her confusion, she was oddly relieved. Her hope of breaking free from that prison and saving her people grew. She just needed to remain patient and faithful.

\*\*\*

During the next week, the gray-eyed general secretly watched the princess paint, sing, sleep, eat, and tell stories to the growing light in the night sky. At times, she spoke as though the light were speaking back, although the shark could never hear anyone else but her; all he noticed was the strong wind that seemed to pick up anytime she spoke to the light.

He knew he would need to leave soon to report what he'd found to the shark king. The king would surely be happy to hear the princess wasn't responsible for the light in the sky, but he wouldn't be pleased about the rest—that she was growing more vibrant each day and appeared to be happy, not broken; that more plant life was sprouting up around the enclosure, as if the princess's energy was causing it all to thrive.

The gray-eyed general knew the shark king would want the princess dead after he heard the general's report.

And for some odd reason, this bothered the gray-eyed shark.

He found himself enjoying the many colors springing up inside and outside the princess's enclosure, and he knew deep down that he was falling for the princess. Desperately unsure of what to do, the gray-eyed general continued to delay his return to the dark kingdom. He would have to choose, and how could he do that when the choice was between the crea-ture to whom he owed his life and the one to whom he felt his heart opening?

*She doesn't even know who I am. Could she ever feel for someone like me the way I feel for her?*

\*\*\*

The princess knew the gray-eyed shark general was spying on her.

One day, she'd decided she would take a nap before the evening sky appeared, and not long after she'd closed her eyes and drifted away, she'd been awoken by the sound of the latch opening and the door creeping open, then shut again. She'd lain perfectly still with her eyes closed.

She'd suspected that someone was watching her, and now this suspicion was confirmed.

Slowly, she peeked from beneath her eyelids, and there was the gray-eyed general, wandering around inside the enclosure, not taking his beautiful gray eyes off of her for long. She remembered those gray eyes. She remembered seeing them when she was a young girl and then again when she'd been captured.

As she watched, he examined her art on the walls, looked at her for a few long moments, and then crept out. Something in her heart longed to speak to this mystery soldier, yet she also knew he worked for the shark king, so she had no reason to trust him. Still, she felt something for him that she hadn't felt before, but she ignored it.

She had other things to focus on and could not be distracted.

## Chapter 13

# Good to Meet You

**One evening, as the princess talked to the captivating light in the night sky, now grown so much bigger, she felt hypnotized by the evening and the cold, crisp air whispering nighttime songs.** The night sky was gloomy with clouds scattered over the black canvas, and raindrops sprinkled from the clouds. The princess closed her eyes, listening to the sprinkling rain hitting the calm ocean surface. She loved the sound and began swaying in unison with her surroundings.

\*\*\*

Nearby, in the shadows of the rock in the enclosure, the gray-eyed general also listened to the sweet lullabies in the air. They were hypnotizingly pleasant and alluring, and he began to sway sleepily.

***

The princess woke when she felt a strong breeze nudge against her. Had she fallen asleep? She focused on her breathing as she came fully awake, and the thought of the gray-eyed soldier crossed her mind. What was he doing at that moment?

Suddenly she heard a noise directly beneath her. Deciding to investigate, she moved swiftly off the top of the rock and into the water, toward the noise. Listening, she moved carefully forward, then froze—there, propped in a little crevice of the rock, the gray-eyed general lay asleep.

*Why is he here?* she thought. *Should I wake him? Is this my chance to make a run for it?*

Uncertain of what to do, she moved out of his direct line of sight in case he woke, then sat silently, waiting.

***

With no idea of how much time had passed, the gray-eyed general shook himself from his unexpected nap, careful to not make too much noise. His heart pounded loudly in his ears. Did the princess know he was there? How long had he been asleep? He tried to listen for the princess, but his own pulse beating in his ears made him feel panicked. It was time to leave the prison.

\*\*\*

*Say something*, the princess thought. Butterflies fluttered in her stomach, and she couldn't make herself speak.

The shark moved toward the prison entrance—now was her chance. She moved into the open.

Their eyes met. A million things she could say raced through her mind, but she still couldn't find her voice. She watched his chest rise and fall and fully surveyed his entire physique—strong, muscular build, skin covered with battle scars.

He moved toward her, never taking his gray eyes off hers.

"I . . . uh . . . ," he stuttered.

She watched his eyes, waiting for him to speak.

"Uh . . . uh . . . ," he stammered again. "Your Highness—good to meet you." He fled past her.

By the time the princess decided to speak, the shark had reached the enclosure door. "Wait!" she shouted.

\*\*\*

He froze with his back to her, his hand on the latch.

"What were you doing?" she asked softly. "Why are you here?"

He couldn't believe she was speaking to him. What should he do? He contemplated rushing out the door, never to return, but he knew that would certainly mean death for the princess. And his heart no longer wanted that. It wanted something else now—something he never imagined he would want.

He slowly turned. She was just a few feet away from him, watching him. He searched his mind for an appropriate response.

"Forgive my intrusion," he said. "I originally came here on business for the new king. I was to report on whether you were the reason the new light is in the night sky. But—" He searched for the words, fidgeting nervously. "I found myself drawn to you in a way I have never experienced before. I was taught my whole life to hate you, but there you were, bearing your soul—I began to feel like I also had a soul again."

He couldn't believe he was being so honest. Something had come over him—he knew he had to continue.

"I'm sorry that I violated your privacy and that I ever doubted you. I will return to the dark kingdom, but I will never speak of any of this, and you will be safe."

He watched her face, but he couldn't tell what she was thinking. Would she speak or remain silent?

Suddenly she straightened. "You are forgiven. I have not been all the way honest either."

The shark frowned. What did she mean?

"I know you have come in here while I was supposed to be asleep. I knew you were watching me, but I didn't lie or pretend to be anything but myself. The bearing of my soul was all real."

Amusement flashed through the gray-eyed shark. She'd known he was there. A slight smile curved his lips. "Okay, Princess. Thank you for your kindness."

He turned to leave, but before he could, the princess said, "You don't have to go! I'm sure you're camped somewhere around here, and your rations have to be getting low. I have plenty here; please stay and join me for a meal."

The gray-eyed shark knew he should leave. But he accepted the princess's invitation.

*Chapter 14*

# Memories

"Sir, still no word from the general, and the light in the sky continues to grow! Should we be concerned?" asked the third-in-command.

More than a week and a half had passed, and the shark king expected his general to have returned by now. Frustration grew in him as more and more questions about the light in the night sky arose in his mind. He dared not say how desperate he was becoming to know what the growing ball of light was.

He glared at the soldier, standing in front of him and awaiting his orders. "Travel quickly to get an update from the general," he said. "Report back to me immediately. Go."

"Yes, sir!" shouted the soldier as he exited the study.

The shark king stared at the door, after him. He had searched every book in his study and could not find anything on the growing light in the night sky. The only remaining option he could think of was to ask the mermaid queen. She was highly intelligent and had traveled much of the sea in her younger days—she might know something about this mystery. He'd have to risk telling her about it.

\*\*\*

In the dungeon, the queen lay on her cot, staring up at the disgusting ceiling of her cell. She was thinking about what she'd overheard a few evenings before when the guards, changing shifts, had clearly assumed she'd been asleep and had been careless.

They'd quietly discussed a light in the night sky that was growing large like the sun. She hadn't been able to believe what she was hearing. Many, many years ago, she'd heard the legend of such a fire in the night sky. It was said to appear at times of great awakening and change.

After hearing the guards' discussion, the queen slept better than she had been sleeping and felt lighter in her energy than before. Something had shifted in the universe, and it was good.

For the first time in a while, the mermaid queen was hopeful of the future.

As she lay on her cot, she heard someone enter the dungeon; her ears had grown sensitive to the sound of unlatching hooks and locks. She stiffened as approaching footsteps echoed in the halls.

*Only one guard*, she thought. *What could he want?*

She closed her eyes and listened as the footsteps grew closer and then stopped outside her cell. A familiar scent wafted through the air. She knew it was her old friend standing there in silence.

"What's the matter?" she asked, her tone condescending. "Feeling a little desperate, my king?"

She opened her eyes and slowly rose from her cot. Her eyes locked on the shark's through the bars as she moved toward him.

He grunted. "So you have heard the news, then?"

The queen stared at him intently. "I have heard passing rumors between your ignorant soldiers." She'd already imagined this moment and understood the angle from which she needed to approach the current circumstance— an angle that would get her out of the cell and into the open, where she could see this ball of light for herself. The defeat in the shark's tone told the queen she had ammo, so she took a shot. "I suppose you would like to know what I know about this new mystery?"

He paused, then nodded.

"I can help you," continued the queen, "but first, you must release me from this dungeon and give me a room in the castle."

After a tense moment, he said firmly, "*Done.*" He

walked away without another word.

When the mermaid queen was finally brought out of the dark dungeon, she was surprised by what she found and how much everything had changed. But the walls of her home, releasing a faint glow from the magic rocks in the castle's foundation, would always be the same, even beneath all the new decor.

While she waited for a room to be prepared for her, the queen temporarily lived in a study near the main library at the top of the castle. It appeared to be unoccupied, with a few scattered books lying around and nothing else. She was allowed to bathe and received new dark garments to replace her torn and tattered clothes. The new clothes did not have gold in them—because she had refused to rule next to the shark king, she assumed. Her beauty, however, remained radiant, despite the peasant clothing she was given, and she could tell that each creature crossing her path was filled with admiration, though they still tried to avoid her.

She was soon taken by two servants to the library, which was now the new king's special room. As the two large doors opened, revealing the amazingly restored library, the queen couldn't restrain a gasp. The rest of the castle had been torn apart and decorated in such a depressing manner, but here was this room, so beautifully preserved. The doors locked shut behind her, startling her. She moved forward farther into the room.

She examined the shelves, pulled out books, and

smelled them. She traced her fingers over the books as she walked by them—then realized the shark king was standing at the other end of the room.

"Did you get everything you desired?" asked the shark.

The queen smirked, continuing to move quietly along the wall of books. "To honestly answer that question would offend you, so I will just say that I did get the temporary things I needed to clean up, and I thank you for that."

A moment passed as she continued to trace her fingers up and down the rows of books, reading each title, smiling gently at some of them as they brought up old memories.

The shark king stepped forward. "Do you remember when we were just kids and you and I would read all day?"

The queen stopped moving.

"I would watch you when you were engulfed in your favorite stories," the shark continued. "I felt like I was watching them unfold in your eyes. You got lost in the stories, like I did. Do you remember?"

The shark's question surprised the queen; she'd assumed they'd get straight to the point about the light in the night sky. But his voice had a gentleness that she had never heard before, and the old books paired with his words brought a cascade of memories flooding into her mind.

She hadn't spent much time in the library after she had married the mermaid king, because she'd been deeply involved with the kingdom after that. She'd only found herself in the library when she was looking for the princess—who always seemed to be reading. But now, the shark's question transported her back in time; she remembered sitting in this room, across from the young adopted shark prince, wanting to be near him. It was a special memory of a different time, before she'd so deeply loved the mermaid king, one she remembered with fondness and kept locked away in her heart.

"Yes, I do remember," she answered softly. She felt herself blushing as she turned toward the shark king.

He moved toward her.

*He's a shell of the creature he once was*, the queen thought as he neared her. He remained strong and rugged, but an emptiness consumed him, and she could feel it.

"I have always thought you were beautiful, my queen," he said, "inside and out. I have but one regret, and it will remain until the end of my days—I regret not telling you how I felt before you became someone else's."

At his words, she looked downward, and just as she did, he stopped, his chest inches away from her bent head. Her heart broke for the shark king. They had loved each other long ago, and she had let that love go. He had not.

"I am deeply and truly sorry for all the pain I have caused you, my queen." He began to stumble over his words, trying to keep his composure.

The queen heard his breathing quicken and could feel him tighten up in defense. She gently touched her head to his chest. He froze, then continued speaking.

"I will pay for my actions in this life or the next. Just know that in the next, I hope I claim you before he does, because you and I are connected eternally, in one life or another."

Tears began to fall down the queen's cheeks, dripping onto the floor. How could she withstand the many emotions she suddenly felt? She pushed away from the shark king and left the library, returning to her room.

The exchange shook the queen to her core. She had to rest, to regroup.

\*\*\*

Meanwhile, the shark king's third-in-command sped toward the prison enclosure.

He had waited for an opportunity to prove himself to the king, and this would be it. When the shark king had still been the mermaid king's general, the third-in-command had worked hard for him, rising in the ranks right next to him, always remaining more loyal to the shark than to the mermaid. But when the kingdom was finally overthrown, he'd been disappointed he was not made the shark king's new general. He knew nothing of this gray-eyed soldier who had taken the job he desired.

But he would not let it bother him.

Selfish, greedy, and happy to do the dirty work, he'd

graciously accepted the role of third-in-command, hoping one day he would rise higher. Maybe this was his chance to start.

*What will I find at the prison?* he anxiously thought as he drew near his destination.

# Chapter 15

# Blooming Love

**The princess gathered fruits for herself and the gray-eyed shark in her enclosure.**

The shark sat comfortably on the floor, resting on a large, tattered cloth blanket she had spread out next to her bed, and watched her carefully handle the fruits and vegetables, as if they were alive and breathing. She took each one in her hand, seeming to admire their unique differences and beauty. He remembered her doing this with the flower, when he'd watched her long ago when they were younger. He admired her ability to see such simple beauty, especially after experiencing her tremendous loss.

He'd pondered this thought the night before and considered his own choices he'd made after losing his family. The princess made him *feel* again, or at least want to try to feel again.

She seemed to finally decide to start with three beautiful fruits that burst at the seams with amazing flavor and colors. He had eaten the fruits before, but not peeled open, revealing their beautiful, delicious insides. Much of the food in the dark kingdom was all mashed together—quantity over quality was the motto in that place.

"Your boss has fed this prisoner well, despite his vicious reputation," the princess joked as she sipped the juice out of the purple fruit in her hand.

The gray-eyed general remained quiet, unsure of how to engage with the princess. He simply smiled and attempted to eat the fruit the same way she was. He struggled with all three of them, although he did enjoy what he could get down.

The princess chuckled. "Have you ever had any of these? You must have—this came from your kingdom's supply."

The gray-eyed general wiped the juice from his lips. "A very long time ago I did, but for much of my life, food has been prepared in a way that's easy to feed to masses—mashed together, with no regard for the beauty of the food. Your supply is handpicked." He took another bite. "I have never stopped to appreciate each piece of food that I put into my body."

She smiled as she finished up the last of the fruit. Then she arranged a buffet of different foods and encouraged the gray-eyed shark to sample each of them. They laughed and joked over each piece of food and told each other stories.

The daytime sky had long vanished, and the brightly lit night sky was above them. The princess grabbed a couple of pieces of carrot fruit and prompted the gray-eyed general to follow her to the surface. On the boulder, they propped themselves up and lay there together, staring directly above them at the beautiful light, now almost fully grown into a sphere.

\*\*\*

The third-in-command arrived at the gray-eyed soldier's camp shortly after sunset. There was no sign of anyone around, so he assumed the general was at the enclosure, spying on the princess, since the light in the night sky would soon be appearing.

Then he heard faint laughter in the distance. Confused and curious, he moved in the direction of the noise. As he stealthily approached the prison's large entrance, he found an abundance of glowing plant life surrounding the enclosure, which startled him. He could hear the princess talking—and occasionally also the new general. His heart raced. Why was the general in there speaking with the princess? He had to see with his own eyes what was going on.

He glanced inside the enclosure. Inside, his comrade and the princess were eating food, laughing, sharing stories, and stealing glances at each other. His heart beat wildly, so loudly he could hear it—he was afraid *they* would hear it. Trying to slow his heart rate and his breathing, the soldier watched the two eat and talk and eventually swim to the surface and climb out onto the giant rock.

He didn't need to see more—he had plenty to report back to the shark king.

Excitement flowed through his veins. This would be the end of the gray-eyed general and the beginning of his own promotion.

The soldier hurried back toward the dark kingdom.

\*\*\*

As the princess and the gray-eyed general lay on the rock, staring at the mysterious bright light in the night sky, the princess reached over to give the shark his piece of carrot fruit and lightly brushed her finger against his. She blushed and giggled a little.

The breeze was strong and wrapped them both in its massive blowing arms.

The princess slowly bit into her carrot, closing her eyes as if she were reminiscing about a different time. The shark watched her do this, admiring her beauty. The light from above glowed down on her, and she was even more breathtaking than he'd previously thought. He could think of no other place he would rather be than right there next to her.

She opened her eyes and found him staring at her. He smiled and returned his gaze to the almost-full ball of light in the sky. She appreciated his strong silence and found comfort in his company, but beyond this, something inside the princess ached for him, and she could no longer deny it as she looked at him in the light of the night. His soft gray eyes examined the sky as he bit into the fruit. She watched as the juices exploded into his mouth and a pleased expression appeared on his face. She longed for more moments like this one.

The breeze picked up, and she moved closer to the gray-eyed general. He wrapped his arm around her and pulled her close, pressing what was exposed of her smooth skin against his. Neither of them knew what was happening between them, but neither could deny the chemistry either. The breeze swaddled them, twirling them into a cocoon of pure feeling. Their hearts beat together, as if as one. He finished his piece of fruit and glanced back to the princess; she stared at him in a way that connected their souls.

He saw a beautiful sunrise in her big, bright eyes. She saw a dazzling sunset in his. Something had grown between them, and they both had an idea of what it was.

It was love.

He gently placed his free hand under her chin and moved closer to her face. Her heart exploded, and her eyes stayed locked on his; she thought the contact felt right, and she didn't hesitate to lean in as well. The moment their lips touched, an energy pulse vibrated off of them and the light above them pulsated in a way it never had before.

Their two opposite hearts had collided in love, and another shift had occurred in the universe.

# Chapter 16

# The News

**The mermaid queen sat on the balcony of her new study, staring out at the big light in the night sky.** She couldn't believe how beautiful it was, and how bright, lighting up everything below. Seeing it with her own eyes strengthened her hope that it signaled a change in her kingdom's fate, and she broke down in tears, missing her family.

She had no idea what the great awakening would be like, but she hoped a solution would present itself soon.

\*\*\*

The shark king watched the queen from a balcony adjacent to hers. Her sorrow seemed to feed something in him, as if it were fuel. Revolts were occurring all over the kingdom, and the new king felt he might soon find himself without a home again.

If the light in the night sky did not leave.

He continued to watch the queen cry, then finally decided he would try to get some rest. The day had been filled with emotion, and he needed to clear his head to figure out his next step. He lay down that night feeling uneasy, which made it impossible to sleep for a long time.

Around midday the next day, his third-in-command came storming into the chamber, startling him awake.

"My king, forgive my rudeness, but this cannot wait. I have news you need to hear!"

The shark king shook sleep from his eyes, sat up in his bed, and stared at the soldier. The third-in-command hadn't been gone long, so the shark king hoped for a good report.

"Go ahead," the king grunted.

The third-in-command reported all he'd seen, including the gray-eyed general's visit to the princess and the glowing plant life outside the enclosure.

The king sat in silence as he listened, stunned by the news. When the soldier finished, the king whispered, "Well done," his voice thick with utter disbelief. After a moment, finding himself unable to breathe, he shouted, "*Leave me!*"

The soldier quickly exited as the shark king leapt out of bed, angry and baffled. The princess and his general—how could this be?

*She must have put a spell of some sort on him*, he thought.

A sense of betrayal screamed in his mind, and with each breath he took, anger grew inside him.

"I will kill them," he said. He prepared to travel to the prison.

\*\*\*

The princess and the gray-eyed general woke to find they had slept through much of the day after falling asleep in each other's arms the night before.

The shark smiled and played with the princess's beautiful purple hair. "Did you sleep well?" he asked her gently.

"Yes," she whispered, still in awe of what had happened between them.

He had stolen her heart, and she had stolen his.

They stared at each other, wishing the moment could last forever, but they both knew the reality of the situation. As the princess adjusted her body, she suddenly brushed across the stone hidden beneath the gray-eyed shark's shirt. She gasped and sprang away in horror, remembering the true power of the stone.

The shark had completely forgotten that he was wearing the stone and about the darkness it had caused. He ripped the stone from around his neck and gripped it in his hands.

The princess fought back tears, staring at his hands.

"I'm sorry—I am so sorry," the shark general whispered.

Without responding, the princess rolled off of her rock and swam down to the rations to make something to eat. The gray-eyed general followed and watched her in silence. He was in love with the creature in front of him, and he would do anything to protect her now.

"We should run away together!" he said suddenly.

The princess froze, dropping the fruit she was holding.

"I love you," the gray-eyed shark continued. "And the shark king will have our heads when he finds out."

The princess listened as her new love poured his heart out to her.

The shark moved closer. "We can go to the dark kingdom, rescue your mother, and leave for good. I know the sea very well and can find us somewhere to live in peace for the rest of our days. I'm so sorry for my role in all of this—I am so sorry for everything."

The princess appreciated that he'd mentioned her mother, but she knew the shark king would never let them run away, and that even if they did, they would never be safe or able to live freely.

"My sweet love," she said as she moved next to him and took his hand. "We cannot run—we must fight. The only way we can be free is if we fight."

The gray-eyed general cringed at the idea of fighting the shark king, but he knew the princess was worth it.

They both sat down to eat and tried to develop a plan of attack on the dark kingdom, but their planning quickly turned into laughing, joking, hugging, and kissing one another. They both enjoyed each other so much, they didn't want to dampen the moment with reality.

However, the princess kept thinking about the stone, which she'd noticed the gray-eyed shark had shoved in his pocket earlier. She wondered whether it would kill her if she broke out into full song. She hadn't sung during the time she'd spent with the gray-eyed general, unsure of how he'd feel if she did. With these thoughts on her mind, the princess began to hum. She needed to distract herself, so she asked her new beau, "Would you like to paint something?"

"Yes, I'll try," the gray-eyed general said. When she'd started humming just then, he'd felt the stone begin a low pulse in his pocket, and not wanting to tell her this since he knew the stone could cause her a lot of pain, he hoped the painting would distract her from humming.

He watched as she mixed together different fruits, vegetables, and seasonings to create the colors. She explained everything she was doing to him as though he were a child learning in school for the first time. He imagined her as a mother—so soft and nurturing. She was not only beautiful but extremely intelligent and kind. Any child would be lucky to call her Mom. He had never thought of anyone this way and usually had no interest in children, but all at once, the idea of marrying her and having a family seemed appealing.

When the colors were mixed, he helped her carry them over to an empty wall in the enclosure. The princess started humming again, and the general felt the rock in his pocket vibrate more intensely.

"How should I begin?" he asked as he stared at the blank wall.

The princess smiled and kissed the shark on his cheek. "However you want," she said lightly. "The fun in creating is that there are no rules, no laws, no boundaries—only the limitless possibilities of the mind."

The shark general felt lost in those words, staring at the wall. He slowly reached for a color, unsure of which to use first, then settled on red and took it in his hands.

The princess started humming louder, and the stone jumped around in the general's pocket even more.

*I have to get her away from it and find a way to get rid of it,* he thought.

As charmingly as possible, he suggested that he wanted to surprise her with whatever he decided to paint and that she should go find something to do until he was done. Giggling and blushing, the princess agreed and swam to the far end of the enclosure, on the other side of the enormous rock.

*Is he just being sweet?* she thought. She could tell the gray-eyed general experienced discomfort when she hummed—she'd noticed him reach for his pocket when she began and hurry along their conversations or interrupt her. She hoped he had the best intentions, but she kept her guard up—after all, he still had the weapon that killed her father in his pocket.

She tidied up while he worked on the other end of the enclosure, peeking around the rock occasionally to watch him as he focused on unleashing something from deep within himself. This excited her. Her mother and father had taught her that art could heal some creatures for whom song or other avenues of healing didn't work. She wondered if the shark was healing. He'd spoken to her about his gloomy childhood and losing his family, about how he'd met the shark king, and about how the shark king had raised him after saving his life. He'd lived much of his life in the dark with his heart in chains, and she hoped that with each stroke of paint on the wall, he was releasing it all.

The princess sprawled out on the blanket next to her bed, staring upward. Since they'd slept much of the day, the night sky would descend soon, and the beautiful ball of light would hopefully arrive. She decided to go up to her spot on the rock and watch the daytime sky greet the night before it went to bed.

On the rock, she watched as the breathtaking night sky blew thousands of goodbye kisses in the form of stars to the departing daylight. One by one, the stars appeared, bright and luminous, hanging ever so gracefully in the black abyss. Her heart began to pound as the wind picked up—the sign of her friend's arrival.

But something was different.

She searched the sky and waited in silence, but the light did not appear. Confused, she sat frozen, still waiting. Then she remembered her friend telling her that even if she couldn't see it, it still existed. That thought comforted her.

Appreciating the beauty of the evening, the princess began to sing the tune she'd been humming.

The song echoed along the walls of the enclosure, and the gray-eyed general's stone began to shake violently, pulling him out of his concentration. He'd planned to get rid of the stone when she was distracted, but he'd forgotten when he'd started painting. He spun around, searching for the princess to tell her to stop. Though the stone had vibrated when she'd sung earlier, while he was still just spying on her, it was much stronger now. Her voice was angelic, but he knew the power of the stone—it could drain her of her life. He had to get rid of it.

But first, he had to make her stop singing.

***

The shark king moved as if at the speed of light toward the princess's prison. He had to see with his own eyes what was going on.

After hearing the soldier's report, the king had gathered his necessary weapons, put his third-in-command in charge, and left the castle, and he hadn't slowed his pace since. The dark, calm ocean was easy to navigate now that no one was ever outside; he could move as quickly and violently as possible, and no one was in his path.

The new king understood it was ludicrous to expect the princess to obey him. But that was exactly what he expected his general to do—especially after all the shark king had done for him. How could the gray-eyed shark betray him this way?

The shark king felt more hurt than he could understand.

Someone had to pay.

## Chapter 17

# Fearless

**Where was the princess?**

The gray-eyed general hadn't realized the sun had set and been replaced by the night sky. He'd become so connected to his art that for a moment, nothing existed except himself and the paint splattering onto the wall. The princess was still singing, and the stone was still vibrating in his pocket. He realized the princess was in the same spot in which they had fallen asleep the night before.

The princess no longer feared the stone—she no longer feared anything. She was free in her heart and would not let anything or anyone convince her otherwise.

She surveyed the night sky as she sang, expecting to see her still-absent friend, the light in the sky, appear. Even without the new light, the night seemed bright as the princess sang her words of love. The space around her felt charged with power as she delighted in the electricity in the air. Her voice grew louder as she felt the energy build up at the base of her spine.

Suddenly, strong hands yanked her body into the water. Her breath driven from her, she stopped singing, trying to push away from whomever had grabbed her. Turning, she faced the gray-eyed soldier, who panted hard as he stared at her. Had he turned on her?

"You can't sing with this here!" he yelled. He held the flickering stone in front of her face. "I have to get rid of it, but until then, you have to refrain from singing like that. We saw what it can do—I will *not* lose you that way!"

The princess immediately regained her composure and smiled, gazing deep into the shark's gray eyes. Without speaking, she took his hand and led him back to where she'd been singing. The energy continued to build up in her body.

She would show him what it was like to be fearless.

The gray-eyed shark started to speak again, but something about the way she held his hand and the look on her face told him she knew exactly what she was doing. He followed in silence.

\*\*\*

As the shark king approached the prison, he instantly noticed the glowing plant life that had grown to enormous sizes around the enclosure and brightened the night. The light in the evening sky had not appeared yet, though it had been dark for some time now, and the shark king began to feel hopeful again.

Maybe the light had run its course and he could continue ruling his dark kingdom with no more distractions.

Plans flooded his mind—how to contain the glowing plant life, how to kill his general. He would not let him live if the report he'd received was indeed true.

He would make an example of his general.

He pondered how he would approach the upcoming situation. Should he move in fast to get his answers or sit back and watch? As easy as watching seemed, the anger coursing through his body could prove difficult for him to withstand. But maybe the third-in-command had been inaccurate and his gray-eyed partner hadn't betrayed him but was acting on a plan that would help the shark king. He wouldn't know until he saw with his own eyes, so he silenced his mind and moved forward.

He felt a vibration around him as he neared the prison entrance. The wind was howling, and he couldn't hear anything as he moved closer. The unexpected thought that his general and the princess could have already escaped flashed through his mind.

*What would keep them there if my general has truly turned on me?* he thought.

Panic gripped the king, and he moved quickly to the

door. He looked inside.

Bright colors covered the prison's walls. The king jumped back in disbelief—the princess had no paints. How could she have painted the walls? He couldn't believe his eyes.

\*\*\*

Hurricane-force winds swirled around the princess and the general as she sang her beautiful song of love.

The gray-eyed general removed the stone from his pocket and held it firmly in his hand. The night before, as she'd slept in his arms, he'd decided he would never let anyone or anything harm her again. He would dedicate his life to her, if she would allow it. But could he stop the stone from hurting her if she kept singing?

The night seemed so bright, though the ball of light was still nowhere to be seen. The princess felt energy intensifying inside her. She squeezed the gray-eyed general's free hand and felt energy pulsing through his body from the stone in his other hand. She looked into his eyes and felt comforted and safe as she sang.

They could both feel the stone's energy growing, but they didn't feel drained—they felt powerful and uplifted.

The general's body relaxed as he released his fear of what could happen. He began to accept the princess's words, and in that moment, nothing else mattered.

\*\*\*

The shark king battled the hurricane-force winds while trying to see what was happening inside. He decided to enter the enclosure, whether the general and the princess were there or not. He was their king, and they would bow down and obey him, or they would die.

After he turned the key and entered, he glanced around the space. He waited to see if they would appear at the sound of the door opening, but he heard and saw nothing. The sweet smell of fruit lingered in the air, and the walls were full of paint. Neither the princess nor his general was anywhere in sight, but the king assumed they were near—fresh, half-eaten fruits and vegetables scattered the ground.

The wind danced around him. Suddenly, he thought he could hear talking from above. As he moved quickly toward the sound, he realized his stone was suddenly vibrating much more than before.

He knew in his gut it was the princess singing.

Above the water, he spotted both of them, staring into each other's eyes as the princess sang. He could tell they hadn't seen or heard him, so he knew he had the advantage. As he watched them stare at each other, he waited for the ball of light to appear, but it was still nowhere in the sky. The princess's hair had grown long since he'd last seen her—the shark king couldn't believe how beautiful she was.

She looked like her mother.

At this realization, the shark king's heart ached. He envied the gray-eyed general—not for winning the princess's heart, but for simply being able to share his heart with *someone*. The shark king would give anything to go back and switch places with the young mermaid king, to offer his heart to the young mermaid queen first. Life would have been entirely different.

***

The mermaid queen roamed the empty halls of the castle. She felt that everyone avoided her and that the servants were ashamed to look her in the eyes.

*I have to find out more about what's happening*, she thought as she continued roaming, trying to talk to soldiers and servants she met. After several failed attempts, she decided to find something to eat and headed toward the kitchen.

When she found it, she realized it was in much worse condition than she'd imagined. It looked as though it hadn't been cleaned in years, with old food crusted and caked in various places and hundreds of smelly dishes scattered everywhere. The food she found was the bland, mushed-together, almost-tasteless food they fed her in the dungeon, which she had no desire to eat. But wouldn't the various ingredients, not yet combined, be stored somewhere? She continued searching, and finally she found a few pieces of fruit in a back pantry. She grabbed them, and when she turned, she noticed a small light coming from the patio doors. She quietly approached, listening for guards. Hearing nothing but the wind, she slowly pushed forward through the double doors onto the large patio area.

A younger dolphin creature sat on the patio, eating quietly and staring at the night sky above. She jumped up at the sound of the door opening and slowly turned her head. She stared at the queen, shock widening her eyes. When she started to speak, the queen hushed her.

"Sit, sit—may I please join you?" asked the queen.

The young creature glanced around, as if looking for anyone in sight, then nodded.

"Yes." The dolphin returned to her food, keeping her eyes down. She was eating the mush food, and the queen thought she didn't appear to enjoy it much.

The queen started to crack open one of the fruits she'd found, and the young creature slightly lifted her head at the sound of it. The queen carefully peeled away the fruit's skin, split it into two pieces, and offered a half to the young creature.

"No, miss," the young dolphin whispered. "I am not allowed."

The queen lifted the young dolphin's face. "Neither am I, so let's do it together."

The dolphin smiled and took the fruit. She slowly sniffed it and looked at it closely, as if it were the first time she'd ever had the fruit.

"Thank you," she whispered.

The queen smiled and enjoyed her fruit with the young dolphin. It was nice to have the company and not be ignored. They stared up at the night sky and talked about the light that had recently appeared, though it was now absent. The young creature explained how the new king had announced that he was responsible for the light in the night sky but that no one believed him—everyone just feared his power. She spoke of battles that had ensued on the streets while the queen had been locked away in the dungeon; many creatures had tried to sing, had encountered the stones' terrible power, and were now fighting to regain their freedom. The queen remembered seeing the large stone in the palace and the small stones worn by each person she interacted with, and she felt immense sadness as she learned more about them. The young dolphin spoke of losing her mother and father as they'd tried to fight the law of darkness and how she'd ended up a servant.

"I miss the days you and our late king were in charge," the dolphin said softly. "We all took those days for granted."

As they spoke, the wind howled around them, growing stronger the longer they talked. The queen could feel a unique energy in the air, and she knew something was happening.

The young creature's stone around her neck began vibrating. Alarmed and unsure of what was happening, they both sat in silence, waiting as the air around them grew more and more charged. The young creature removed the stone from around her neck and placed it on the table. They watched it as it flickered with the energy in the surrounding water.

The young creature grabbed the queen's hand in fear.

\*\*\*

At the same time, many miles away, the princess finished her song.

"I love you," sang the princess.

"I love you," the gray-eyed general suddenly sang back to her.

The princess couldn't believe her ears. Tears burst from her eyes.

The shark dropped the stone, now vibrating crazily between them, and he pulled her close, staring at her with the fire of a thousand suns. For the first time in his life, he wanted to sing, so he continued.

"My love, my life," he sang. "I'm forever yours—will you be my wife?"

As the tune left his lips, an energy field burst upward from his body and toward the sky, where there was still no sign of the ball of light.

\*\*\*

At that instant, in the castle, the queen held the trembling creature, waiting to see what would happen next.

Another energy shift was occurring in the universe.

*Chapter 18*

# The Truth

**The shark king couldn't believe what he was seeing.**

His general was singing, and some type of energy was expanding off his body.

The stone dropped from his general's hand, and the gray-eyed shark pulled the princess close and sang again, asking for her hand. That was it—the shark king had seen enough. Chaotic energy surged through his body. He lunged toward the general and the princess, revealing himself.

\*\*\*

The gray-eyed shark and the princess spun around and froze—the person they'd desperately feared stood directly in front of them.

The gray-eyed general sprang into a defense position, aware of how strong his ruler was, and the princess retreated behind him. The air was electrified as the two sharks stood face to face. The wind howled all around them, and the princess searched for her friend in the sky, but there was still no sign of it anywhere. The shark king stared at his prodigy, and his eyes showed a hatred and fire that the gray-eyed shark had never seen.

"This is how you repay me—after everything I have done for you!" yelled the shark king. "You betray me for this 'song wizard.' I never thought you would be fooled by the magic—but I was wrong. I own you. I would have left you to die if I'd known one day you would repay me this way."

The gray-eyed shark watched the king's movements as he spoke. He felt slight shame—he was very loyal to the king and had not planned for any of this to happen.

"Sir," he said, "nothing I could say to you would change what you saw today. I did not plan this—you have to believe me. I tried to remain focused on our goal, but my heart is bound to the princess's. My king, you of all people should understand that!"

The gray-eyed general knew of the love the shark king had for the mermaid queen—when the gray-eyed shark had been young, the older shark had told him about his love, about the series of events that prevented him from asking the young mermaid on the date he'd already planned. When the gray-eyed shark alluded to these memories, an agonized expression crossed the shark king's face. The king released a frustrated roar.

"I do not care! You were sworn into your position as general, and you have breached your contract. You must now die. And, Princess—you have become even more of a problem than your father, so you will now die too."

"She has done nothing!" shouted the gray-eyed general. "Your problem is with me. She was perfectly herself and did nothing to sway me into this."

The princess fought to keep her breathing calm as she listened to the two sharks speak. She could somehow feel the shark king's pain as she cautiously watched him.

The light was still not in the sky, but something was causing the calm waters of the sea to light up more than before. What was causing the light?

She reached for the general's hand and squeezed it as he defended her. The shark king suddenly abandoned the conversation and ambushed the gray-eyed general, ripping his hand from the princess's and tossing him many feet away. The gray-eyed shark crashed through the prison wall.

The force of the shark king's attack threw the princess backward. She hit her head, and her vision blurred.

Outside the enclosure, the gray-eyed general lay on the glowing plant life, his ears ringing from the crash through the wall. Where had the glowing plants come from? Were they real, or was he seeing things because he'd hit his head so hard? He quickly shook off the attack, turned, and stormed toward the shark king.

Still inside the prison, the princess fought to regain her balance and composure. Her beau charged back through the hole in the wall and crashed into the shark king, lifting him through the water and against another wall.

Through the hole in the prison wall, the princess saw something glowing. She blinked, then looked again. Glowing plant life covered the ground outside the prison. She couldn't believe her eyes—she'd never seen anything like it in her life. This must be why the shark king had said she was an even bigger problem than her father.

Light had found a way, just as her father and the light in sky had said.

The typhoon-like wind crashed around the still waters as the princess helplessly watched the two sharks battle.

\*\*\*

The mermaid queen and young dolphin continued to sit in silence, feeling the high winds and intense energy of the night. A gust of air swept in, swinging the patio door open and startling them both. They turned—the third-in-command stood in the doorway, staring at them.

The young creature jumped up and quickly left with her head down, making no eye contact with the soldier as she scurried away.

The queen's hair flowed freely in the wind, and the soldier stared at her in silence. She sat silently, not moving as he approached her. He finally stopped and sat where the young creature had been sitting before.

"My lady," he said calmly as he looked her in the eyes.

"Sir." She nodded, then returned her gaze to the sky.

"No light in the sky tonight, huh?" the soldier said, almost mockingly. "Must mean the shark king finished the job."

Confused by the comment, the queen turned her head and said, "What job, if I may ask?"

The soldier stared at her in silence, with a large, crooked smile on his face. "No, you may not ask," he said, "but since you did and I am feeling good about tonight, I will be generous and answer."

His arrogance disgusted the queen. She knew this soldier well, as he'd been around when her husband ruled. She'd never spoken to him much, but because he'd risen through the ranks with the then shark general, she'd assumed he was an ideal soldier.

"Let me start by saying your daughter is alive," the soldier continued. "Well, she was the last time I saw her."

The queen's heart rejoiced, but she didn't change her composure.

"She is being held far from here, in a prison," said the soldier. "She was placed there after she watched us kill your husband, her father, with our precious stones."

The queen cringed, thinking of her baby girl witnessing such a thing.

The soldier pulled his stone out from beneath his shirt. It was vibrating and flickering, but the soldier didn't appear to be affected by it.

"Well, my queen, everything was fine until this light appeared in the night sky. Of course, naturally, we assumed it could be your daughter's sorcery, so we sent our newly ranked general to make sure she was not the cause."

The queen listened attentively, trying to keep her nerves under control. She was happy to finally be receiving some information, but it was hard to hear now that she knew her daughter had watched her husband's death.

"Well, he went to the prison, my lady, and has not returned. And that light in the sky just kept growing bigger! The king selected me to go find out what the delay was, and oh, was I surprised by what I found!" He paused as the loudly blowing wind crashed into the palace walls near them. "I was surprised to find our top-ranked general there, engaging with your daughter, clearly in love. Now, it surprised the king, but it did not surprise me that he had fallen for her. She's a song wizard's daughter, and the apple didn't fall far from the tree."

He reached to touch the queen's hair, but she pulled away.

He laughed. "But I think what surprised me most was that *she* appeared to be in love with *him* too."

The queen couldn't believe what she was hearing. Her daughter was alive—and in love?

"This upset the king, as you can imagine, after I immediately reported back what I'd found, and he left here in a blaze, ready to kill them both! And because the night has been upon us for some time now but the ball of light still hasn't appeared, I would say he probably succeeded."

The thought of losing her daughter again after having just found out she was alive was too much for the queen to handle. Tears filled her eyes.

The soldier laughed and rose from the table. "If I were you, I would change my mind about not ruling next to the king. When he returns, there will be no stopping us!"

He left the patio.

The wind kissed the queen's cheeks as she sat, processing all she'd heard. She knew, deep down, she could still feel the special connection to her daughter, so she shook off her fears.

She returned her attention to the night sky, hoping for the ball of light to return or for whatever other magic was still waiting to appear that evening.

*Chapter 19*

# The Moon's Awakening

**The mystery in the night sky awoke not knowing who, what, or where it was.** It was suspended in the deepest, darkest depths of a gigantic black sky. Its physical size was enormous to itself, but from land or in the water, it was barely visible to the naked eye; it appeared to be hundreds of thousands of miles away from the surface below.

The view of the dark sky was breathtaking. The space surrounding the mystery buzzed with energy. Then, without warning, the mystery was flooded with knowledge, and in a flash it understood that it was made up of a hard rock material, that it was a sphere, that the dazzlingly sparkling rocks surrounding it in the sky were called stars, and that it hung above a place called Earth. It could see Earth's land and water stretched out beneath it.

It traveled slowly across the dim sky, feeling pulled into the natural flow of the surrounding universe. It observed and absorbed the information and energies it detected from below, listening to the wonderful wisdom and stories coming from the enchanting stars themselves. They had existed since creation and had seen so many things. They told epic tales of love and war and so many other gifts of life.

The sphere felt all the different energies swirling together to create the stars, those physical representations that expressed themselves. It felt the whole universe and how everything in it was connected. It knew instantly that there were lessons to be learned and wisdom in all experience. Though the stars, land creatures, and sea creatures all experienced the same moment of time, they each possessed a separate conscious perspective. The sphere knew it now had its own perspective and its own lessons to be learned and goals to achieve.

As the large rock in the sky moved and took in everything, it started to notice an imbalance in the energy of the place now directly beneath it. It continued moving, and over the next couple of days, as the sphere traveled, it noticed the same imbalance of energy over the same area.

One evening, as it moved, hidden, in the night sky, it came across the imbalance again, but this time it saw the mermaid princess. The sphere had seen many creatures, but there was something different about this one. A unique kind of energy pulsed from the creature, luring the sphere closer.

It halted directly above the princess's enclosure, in darkness, hidden from sight, and watched and listened.

The mermaid creature was wrapped in a cloud of despair despite her lovely, beaming aura. She began to sing, and all of a sudden, something sparked inside the hard sphere. A fire began deep down in its core, and as the melody continued, the fire grew hotter and hotter. Energy from the singing creature below burst through the atmosphere and into the rock and pulsed through its entire body. It began to vibrate because of the fire growing inside itself, and suddenly the fire created a white glow within the sphere. The sphere felt a warmth it hadn't experienced before, and it knew that it had found the reason for the warmth's absence—no one but the mermaid was singing.

This had to change.

The sphere realized that the mermaid creature had noticed it and was now speaking directly to it. It had never spoken to anyone other than the ancient stars; no one had ever noticed it before this moment. The sphere understood that the creature was female in energy as it listened to the terrible things she had to say. She poured her heart out to it, and as she did, an overwhelming amount of energy burst through the atmosphere again. The vibration inside the sphere grew. It had to speak back to this creature, to whom it was obviously connected.

Knowing it was far too big to speak directly to any creature on the land, including the mermaid, the sphere asked the wind for help, hoping the mermaid would hear its message on the wind waves. If she was meant to hear the words, she would—and she did.

Speaking to the mermaid princess was a joy for the ball in the night sky each night, and it noticed that its warmth and white light grew with each encounter. It also noticed a shift in the energy coming from Earth since it had first appeared in the sky. The ball of light sensed that hope was a strong vibrating energy and could feel it more and more with each passing day. More creatures looked to it, and it could hear others trying to sing.

The sphere chose to share wisdom with the princess every time they spoke, intending to empower her. It could feel its light inside spreading.

When the gray-eyed creature arrived, the sphere of light instantly knew the creature's muddied energy was important. The sphere saw the shark creature watching the mermaid and knew the creature couldn't hear its messages on the wind. It chose not to inform the princess of the new development when they spoke; things would have to unfold naturally between the shark's and mermaid's energies without the sphere's interference. The shark's energy was male, and there was a low, magnetic vibe between him and the princess, of which the sphere could tell they were unaware. It tried to help them by sending lullabies on the wind to help the energy flow.

The moment the two of them finally locked eyes for the first time, the energy between them caused some kind of chain reaction within the rock up in the sky. The vibrating energy force crashed around inside the solid sphere. The light was spreading at a quicker rate through its whole body, and it sensed a new type of energy emerging. It knew that the two creatures were important and watched as they spent time together. The energy between them pulsed into the atmosphere, and the ball of light knew they were falling in love. It watched as the densely energized third-in-command spied and knew there would soon be a battle with darkness. As it continued to watch everything on Earth, it sent whispers of hope on the wind, kissing the cheeks of all those who hoped for better days.

A power was expanding inside the sphere. Then, something out of the ordinary happened for the first time as it traveled the night sky one evening, headed toward the creatures. The gigantic rock was vibrating faster than ever, and it was now a full ball of white light. The sphere had planned to inform the princess of the spying third-in-command creature and warn her that there was a dense energy headed their way, but instead, it found itself in a new place it had never been before.

This place was mesmerizing and dynamic, a place of all creation, the source of the universe. Words were not spoken there; knowledge simply flowed in and out of the area, painting a picture for the sphere. In this place, the sphere saw how all things were intertwined and connected and how everything came from the same source—from *this* source. Immersed in what it was seeing, the large lit-up sphere was unsure of what would happen next. It would have to wait and see.

# Chapter 20

# Love Lost

**The gray-eyed general continued to battle for his life.** He and the shark king exchanged blows, slamming each other into the ground and back into the walls of the enclosure, causing the structure to shake. Blow after blow, they fought with every ounce of energy they had.

The princess attempted to attack the shark king but was thrown a far distance. She landed on her back and hit her head again. Trying to shake off the blow, she lay there, staring at the sky. Only then did she notice that the night sky above was changing—green and blue colors swirled around in it. What was happening? She searched for her friend, who had still not appeared. She reminded herself that even if she didn't see the light in the night sky, it did still exist and always would.

She returned her attention to the two sharks battling ferociously back and forth across the prison. She had to help.

She knew they would have to kill the king.

The two sharks flew through the water, exchanging punch after punch and kick after kick. Every time they exchanged a blow, a burst of light flashed like lightning and was followed by loud thunder. She knew she was fully in love with the gray-eyed general as she watched him fight for her. He was a noble warrior, and the way he fought reminded her of her father. As she watched, he punched the face of the shark king, and the king lost his balance and crashed to the ground. His flickering stone flew from his body and landed on the ground in front of her.

The sharks battled hard as the wind whirled around them. The gray-eyed general grew tired and knew he couldn't fight much longer. He had to try to end the fight—and he knew that meant killing the shark king.

"Why does it have to be this way?" the gray-eyed general shouted as they wrestled. "I did not plan for things to happen this way—you have to believe me!"

By this point, the shark king had no intention of talking about the situation anymore. He wanted the gray-eyed general and the princess dead. The general was a worthy opponent, and the king was growing tired from their battle. He had to finish him quickly.

Suddenly the king noticed the princess regaining her composure and preparing to attack again. He remembered his hidden knife, and he reached for it, making sure the general didn't see. As they struggled, the king pulled out the knife and thrust the blade into the gray-eyed general's side.

The gray-eyed shark screamed in pain.

Adrenaline rushed through the general's body, and he flung the king away as he realized what had just happened. Pain was all he felt, and his energy was disappearing. He grabbed his side where the knife was still lodged, yanked the knife out, and dropped it to the ground.

The princess felt slightly stunned—the general's scream when the shark king had stabbed him had touched the very depths of her soul. She knew he was badly injured. Summoning her training as a fighter, she rushed the king just as the general flung him backward, and she caught him off guard. She punched his face and body. She could tell he was much more tired, and she was able to avoid his counterattacks. Her father had believed she should be able to fully defend herself at any time and had made sure she received training—ironically, the shark king, whom she now fought, had been the one who had trained her, back when he was still her father's general.

The gray-eyed shark hadn't moved since removing the knife from his side, and the shark king laughed and mocked the princess as he picked himself up off of the ground.

"Looks like your love doesn't have what it takes to defend his queen!" he said.

The princess rushed to the gray-eyed shark's side and prompted him to get up, but he seemed unable to. She could tell he was badly wounded and slipping away. Fear crept into the princess's heart, and she searched her mind for some way to help him. She had healing powers, but she knew that the shark king wasn't going to just allow her to heal him.

They needed a miracle, and they needed it fast.

The king laughed, spitting out blood, as the princess tried to think of a solution. She thought back to her time with her father and knew he'd have found an answer quickly. Her hope started to slip away.

Suddenly, she noticed the king's stone flickering on the ground. It had been flickering the whole time, as though it were trying to tell her something.

*A fight song!* she thought.

She had the power within her, but she'd never used a fight song. Could she do it, after what happened to her father? Would it kill her? But what other choice was there? If the stone didn't kill her, the shark king surely would.

She refused to let the fear take over as she searched the colorful night sky for her friend, desperately wishing it were there to empower her.

*Oh well,* she thought. She would have to try—it was their only chance.

As the shark king stood watching and laughing, the princess raised her head to the colorful night sky and sang out for her friend from the bottom of her heart.

\*\*\*

The queen was still sitting on the patio when the blue and green colors appeared in the sky. The little dolphin creature had returned to sit with her after the third-in-command left, and they both couldn't believe what they were seeing. Nothing like that had ever happened in the queen's lifetime, nor, she expected, in any other lifetimes in history.

The weather had become odd. It was as if it were storming, though there was no actual storm. In the distance, flashes of light exploded randomly, followed by what sounded like thunder. What could it be?

The queen could feel a power surging beneath her skin, and she knew deep down that the awakening had begun.

\*\*\*

The large sphere of light in the night sky remained suspended in this new, strange place, where all types of energy frequencies swirled around at different speeds.

Suddenly, the vibrating sphere received knowledge of what these energy frequencies represented. They represented moments of hope and happiness brought about on Earth by the sphere's presence in the sky the past month. The sphere felt the heat of the light vibrating within itself as it watched millions of colors swirl around it. An inexplicable warmth consumed its entire body, and the ball of light felt it was being rewarded for achieving a goal and learning its lesson. Though it felt tremendous gratitude for the experience, the sphere didn't feel it deserved to be rewarded yet.

The princess was tugging at its consciousness—it could feel that something was wrong.

Just as the sphere became aware of the princess's tugging at its core, its surroundings started to shift, as if an eraser were slowly wiping away some of the colors in the sky.

The sphere saw the battle below on Earth.

The giant glowing sphere watched as if through glass as the shark king and the gray-eyed general battled. It saw the princess search the sky and realized no one on Earth could see it, despite its being bigger and brighter than ever before. It longed to show itself, especially after realizing just how empowering its presence was, but the universe had other plans.

"It's her turn to believe again," the universe whispered to the sphere.

As the physical battle went on beneath it, the sphere watched the energy attached to the creatures crash and flow together in the atmosphere. It was as though the giant glowing sphere was watching two different battles, and though the dense negative energy appeared to be winning, the sphere could feel and see a more powerful energy brewing all around, growing stronger and brighter.

And the sphere could tell the princess's energy was the most powerful.

Suddenly, the gray-eyed general was struck by the shark king's knife, and the sphere felt the princess's pain for her love. It watched her search her soul for answers.

"Sing, my dear—sing a fight song!" the sphere willed to her on the wind. "I will sing with you, but you have to sing first, my dear—sing!"

Just as it sent the message out on the wind, the princess turned her head upward, as though she were staring directly at the sphere, and she sang.

\*\*\*

"My friend, where are you to light the night sky? My friend, where are you? I may have to say goodbye. This creature we battle has lost its way. This creature must be defeated, and we need a new day!" the princess sang. Her voice was hauntingly hypnotizing, and the energy behind her words shook the land around them, slightly moving the earth.

As the entire ocean moved a little, the shark king lunged for his stone, which was lit up now and shining brighter with each word that left the princess's mouth.

"You will die, just like your father," screamed the king. "So be it! Your song has no power here, and your friend in the sky has abandoned you—it's nowhere to be found!"

The gray-eyed general knew the shark king's stone had more power than the others. With his last ounce of energy, he reached up and touched the princess as she sang, trying to warn her.

"His stone, my love," he whispered. "It is powerful. You can't—"

She placed a finger on his lips to shush him as she sang. She looked at him with light in her eyes, smiling gently. The gray-eyed shark knew that if they were going to die, she would rather die singing.

And if she was going to sing, she needed all the help she could get.

He grabbed her hand, rested his head back on the glowing plants, and looked up at the beautiful flowing colors in the sky. He listened to her words, swaying gently with them. He knew his time was limited, but the love in his heart was strong, so he gathered every ounce of strength he had left and joined her in singing from the depths of his soul.

"My friend, where are you to light the night sky? My friend, where are you? I have to say goodbye. This creature we battle has lost its way. Help us defeat him so we can see a new day!"

The princess cried as they sang together in love. Electricity shot around them; the princess's hair stood up on the back of her neck.

The shark king couldn't believe what was happening. Deep down, a part of him suffered as he watched the two of them sing the fight song in love. His whole life, a darkness had brewed in him, and the moments he'd had with the young mermaid queen were the best of his life. He had sung once with the queen—one day, he had let his guard down to sing with her. He'd never thought he would, but that day, he was lost in her words and wanted to be a part of them. He knew this is what had happened for his general. He imagined a different time, when the gray-eyed general and the princess could be together—a time without him. Part of him suddenly wanted to quit this fight and retreat into solitude for the rest of his days.

But he couldn't do that.

The stone was vibrating intensely in his hand. He tossed it toward the gray-eyed general and the princess. It landed feet away from them as they sang, and he moved back to watch it do its work.

The crystal appeared to grow as the light inside it burst out over the electrifying energy of the mermaid and gray-eyed shark. The stone was spinning and slowly rising in the air—something he'd never seen it do before. As it spun, it generated a tremendous amount of power, and the king felt himself pushed back farther. He realized the stone was not absorbing the singers' energy, as he'd seen it do before—it seemed to be merging with their energy, creating a vortex of some sort.

Something was different—something was happening!

\*\*\*

The moment the princess and the gray-eyed general's words came together in song, calling out to the giant sphere, the light inside of it became fully lit.

The sphere had been sending messages of hope out on the wind to the entire world as it watched the battle, and the moment the general and the princess sang out together, their energy completed a lesson or a goal of the universe. A weight lifted off the sphere, and it felt free. The magnificent full ball of light burst out into song as the two creatures sang.

"I am here—a new day has come." The sphere's words rode the wind waves to Earth, pushing through the atmosphere. The colors around the sphere melted away, and the glass through which it watched began to break.

\*\*\*

The princess heard the sphere's message, and her heart rejoiced. Then the gray-eyed general's hand went limp, and he stopped singing.

He had passed away into the night.

Tears poured down the princess's cheeks as she squeezed his hand, sobbing silently. She'd thought she would be able to heal him, but it was too late. She knew she had to continue, so after seconds of silence with him, she kissed his cheek and adjusted her body to face the shark king, who had remained at a distance.

The king realized his gray-eyed general, whom he thought of as a son, had just died—because of him. Pushing aside his sudden grief, he considered attacking the princess in the vulnerable moment, but the crystal continued spinning near her, growing in speed, so the king, intrigued, restrained himself and continued watching.

The princess rose and started singing a different song—a song about love. The song-wizard magic inside her bubbled out, and she began to glow as she sang words of love like no one on Earth ever had.

The energy vortex she and her beau had created by singing together had grown, reaching to the night sky. It was breaking through the glass-like energy that concealed the enormous ball of light. The force from the vortex caused the millions of colors to crash around, creating an explosion that slowly revealed the gigantic, fully lit sphere in the night sky. It was hundreds of times bigger than it had ever been.

It was now visible to the entire world.

# Chapter 21

# Transending

**When the sky burst into millions of colors and the full sphere of light revealed itself, the queen knew her daughter had something to do with it—she could feel it.** The mermaid queen and young dolphin creature watched the humongous ball of light in the sky. Around the castle, the queen heard many creatures rejoicing and crying out in joy and saw them hugging one another as they made their way outside to watch the colors in the sky and listen to what sounded like a storm off in the distance. Everyone stood there with their heads turned up toward the perfect ball of light, admiring its beauty. The queen saw the third-in-command running among the people, trying to contain the excitement but clearly failing. It was clear that no one, not even the soldiers, knew what was happening, so they were all simply watching and waiting to see what would happen next.

Suddenly, all their stones began to vibrate violently. The creatures ripped them off and threw them to the ground. The queen knew the power of the stones and what they could do, but still she felt an undeniable urge to sing. The breathtaking sight was enough to lend the queen bravery. She mustered up the courage and began to sing the old light kingdom's anthem. She saw those near her turn toward her, as though they were startled to hear the old song. But soon, many joined in. Eventually, the queen was leading a large group of creatures in singing the light kingdom's song, while the soldiers of the dark kingdom just stood by with no one to lead them.

***

The princess sang with her eyes closed. She didn't care if the shark king attacked her while she sang or if the stone killed her. She was lost in the song, and now she could hear her friend in the sky singing with her even more than before.

She opened her tear-soaked eyes, and the sight of her gigantic friend in the sky stunned her. She lost her balance and fell backward. Fighting back more tears, she felt the wind brush against her cheek and heard the message it carried.

"I am so proud of you, my dear. They are singing again."

The princess felt a surge of power through her heart like never before as she stared at the sight.

A short distance away, the shark king was glaring at the sphere, and the princess could see that he was paralyzed by fear. The stone near her continued to spin. She decided to move toward the king and searched for the words to say to him. He remained frozen. He looked weak and drained, as though the stone were taking his energy instead of hers.

He clearly still hadn't noticed her when the princess stopped a few feet away from him. "Was it all worth it?" she yelled over the strengthening wind.

The shark king jumped, as if her voice had pulled him out of his trance. He sat in silence, glancing between the beautiful purple-haired princess and the giant ball of light.

The wind was so strong again that the princess had to scream her words. "My father once told me that light will always find a way, and today it has! You can kill me, and the next creature, and the next creature, but light always finds a way, and the proof is right there in front of your eyes." She pointed at the full ball of light in the night sky.

He continued to stare at her in silence, as though he was searching for a response. She watched his eyes move back and forth between her, the giant marvel, and the crystal still spinning near the dead general.

"I have but one regret," he said as he met her gaze. "And that is not marrying your mother years ago, before you were born!"

The princess was shocked. How had she never known he felt this way about her mother?

"I should have been the one to ask her out first," he continued. "I would have had a different life—none of this would have happened! I'm not sorry for anything I've done, and I accept whatever fate is in store for me."

Despite all that had happened, the princess still loved the shark king, but she could tell he had given up. She could hear her large, bright friend singing, and she knew that she had to sing with it to end the shark king's reign. She stared at the king while she searched for the words. Finally, she screamed, "I forgive you anyway!" And she began singing again.

The princess's and the sphere's words melted together and flowed across the entire world.

"A new day is here. Have no fear—let the days and nights of darkness now disappear."

The sphere of light increased the volume of its words as they sang, and something began to happen that had never happened before: the earth began to dance. Everything began to violently shake, and for the first time ever, the still waters of the enormous ocean began to move with waves and tides. Energy moved all around the princess, and the wind was more powerful than she'd ever imagined it could be. She and the sphere sang together in perfect unison as the earth danced around, moving the water everywhere. Though she wasn't quite sure how, the princess knew the entire earth was changing forever in that moment.

She stood firm, singing, as the world shifted around her.

The shark king fell to his knees, and his and the gray-eyed general's fast-spinning crystals rose into the air above them.

***

In the kingdom, all the crystal stones also rose into the air, including the large one the shark king had placed in the town's center. They all glowed like the perfect sphere of light in the night sky. All the creatures continued to sing, including many of the soldiers who hadn't fled. The crystals lit up the sky like thousands of stars, and the singing creatures watched them. As they finished their song together, the stones began to shoot off, one by one, into space, exploding as they left the atmosphere. Simultaneously, a beam of energy shot outward and upward like an explosion, reaching every part of the changing world.

***

The energy was so mighty that it blasted the shark king back several feet into the prison enclosure. The princess watched him crash through the walls, sending bricks everywhere, worsening the damage his fight with the general had caused.

The earth stopped dancing, but the ocean water continued to move all around them. The prison, its foundation damaged from the fighting and the earth's dancing, began to fall. As she watched the last crystal stone shoot through the atmosphere and explode, the princess wished for it all to be over. Just as she did, she heard a loud *boom*. The earth directly beneath them began to shake violently. A crack was opening in the earth, and the prison slowly crumbled into it around the shark king. The princess knew he had time to escape, but he just lay there, looking at her. Seconds later, he disappeared beneath the crashing rubble, into the ground.

When the dust cleared, the shark king was gone, covered by the debris from the enclosure and then sucked into the earth as it split from the force of the crash. Nothing was left of the prison except a part of the large rock that the princess had often sat on, though it no longer penetrated the surface above and had mostly disappeared into the ground, with just the top part peeking out. There was no longer any trace of the dark king and his dark prison.

The princess dropped to the ground, out of breath, and returned her gaze to the perfect sphere of light in the night sky. She could see every crack, crevice, and marking on the enormous ball; it sparkled and glimmered like a diamond. Tears rolled down her cheeks as she took in the moment.

All the pain and suffering that had occurred had just ended with the shark king's death. The ocean water was still moving, and the plant life glowed all around the princess. She stared up at the breathtaking sight, then closed her eyes as the wind touched her wet cheeks. Her friend in the sky was singing a beautiful melody that warmed her to the core.

Finally, she moved over to the gray-eyed general, whose body remained in the same place. She kneeled over him, staring at his lifeless body, which shone from the light above. Tears poured from her eyes, and she placed her head on his chest.

"I'm sorry," she whispered.

Suddenly, the light sphere's melody stopped, and the world froze. The princess was instantly in a different place altogether—or at least it appeared to be. She could no longer see her own body, the general, the glowing plant life, or any of her previous surroundings. This place was vibrant and vivid with colors and energy vibrations that flashed around her. It was something she'd only read about as a little girl in her family's vast library—the universe itself, with billions of stars and planets with many suns and many moons. She saw life playing out everywhere, creating so much energy. What was happening? Whatever it was, it was exquisite.

"My dear," boomed her friend's voice all around her. "You have succeeded—you have sparked the light in all life, and you have sparked the light in me! What you see all around you is what you created by opening your heart. In your darkest moment, you somehow reached deep inside yourself to find what is always there, withstanding the tests of time and evil: unconditional love. You loved this creature despite who he was and what he did to you and your people. To see the best in someone even when that person can't, to believe in the light even when you are in the dark, to believe in unconditional love—this is the greatest weapon in the universe. Neither love nor light can be defeated, and love *is* light. Wars, famine, hate, envy, and anger—these things are temporary. They feed fear, and fear is the fuel for darkness. The moment you and the gray-eyed shark sang out to me in unconditional love, you banished fear from your hearts forever! You have reminded the world of a power that cannot be contained."

As her friend spoke, images of many creatures celebrating in all parts of the world flashed into her mind's eye, sent to her by the surrounding energy. She saw that all of the shark king's crystals had been destroyed, and then she saw her mother, singing with the kingdom. The princess's heart exploded with joy at the sight of her mother, and she wanted to celebrate, but she still grieved the death of the gray-eyed general.

"You and I are connected forever now, Princess," continued the sphere's voice. "You helped wake me to my higher purpose, and I thank you for that. I have found my voice, and I will sing for the rest of my days. You will know I am singing, because your calm waters will forever be moved by the energies of my melodies. As a token of my appreciation, I would like to give you something."

The booming voice faded, and a blast of light flashed. When the light dimmed, there stood her father with the universe glowing behind him. The princess couldn't believe her eyes—here he was, full bodied, looking more powerful and vibrant than she'd ever seen him.

"Father!" she cried and, once again able to feel her body, rushed into his arms and pressed her face against his chest. She'd watched him die, but now he was holding her in his powerful arms.

"My daughter." His voice was electrifying. "I am so proud of you and what you have done here. I'm sorry I had to leave you the way I did, but I have been shown by the universe that it was necessary. I have been and will always be proud of you, my love. Your mother and I knew from the moment you were conceived that you were special and that you were meant for important deeds. The love in your heart is more powerful than either of us could have imagined. I need you to be strong and lead the kingdom. You are the rightful ruler, and you have the power to change everything around you."

An image of the glowing plant life flashed before the princess's eyes, and she felt immense energy behind every word her father spoke to her. She wanted desperately to ask him a million questions and never let go of him. She knew he was right. She'd felt all her life, even at a very young age, that she was different.

"Be the light, my child," her father continued. As he spoke, she looked into his beautiful eyes and could see the whole universe looking back. "If you do this, you will be fine for the rest of your days. When you look up in the sky toward this beautiful ball of light, remember that I am with your friend and with all of the universe. When it sings and the water moves, know that I am in those waves crashing up and down and all around. Know that I am in the stars and the sun and the flowers on the ground. I am in every creature, and I am in you. There will be other attempts to block out the light, but you know the truth, and you know what to do. And know that when your time is up in this physical reality, I will be right there to greet you in the next one. I love you. Be happy, my child. Be love."

He kissed her gently on the forehead, smiled at her, and faded away into the swirling energies all around her. She smiled with tears in her eyes.

"Thank you," she said to the sphere.

"One more thing," said the loud voice. "The universe thanks you too. Your father said it perfectly—be love, my dear, and be happy. You will have moments in your life when it may be difficult to remember this message, but it is the truth. Love is the truth. We will always be with you. Thank you for helping me find my voice. Thank you for helping me be love."

Everything around the princess began to vibrate and glow more than ever. She closed her eyes against the brightness.

"Go sing," said her friend's voice as it faded away. When she opened her eyes, everything was back to the way it had been.

She lifted her head from the general's chest and gasped—his beautiful gray eyes, now glinting with a hint of radiant blue, gazed at her.

"You're—" she stammered. "But how?"

He smiled gently, slowly sitting up.

"The universe," he said softly. "I saw everything—my family, your brightly lit friend, your father, the *love*. I'm not sure why the universe gave me another chance, but I do know I won't waste it. I'll use it wisely. And I know one thing for sure: I will love you with everything I have—if you will allow it."

She stared into his eyes, instantly comforted by his words. Though she didn't know how it was possible, this—a second chance with her sweetheart—was the greatest gift the universe could give her. She wrapped her arms around him and squeezed him tightly. He squeezed back, wrapping her tighter in his arms, and her heart smiled.

She leaned toward his ear and whispered, "Of course I will allow it. I will love you forever."

Above them, the sphere of light looked on as their two energies danced in pure love to its melody in the atmosphere.

*Chapter 22*

# Home

**Word traveled quickly about the shark king's defeat and the princess's imminent return, and the queen was so happy to hear the news and anxious to see her daughter again.** She resumed control of her palace, and it wasn't long before the old way of life burst forth once more. Everyone was singing again. Many of the dark kingdom's soldiers broke down at the sight of the full sphere and rejoined the light kingdom, while others, such as the third-in-command, fled. The queen, feeling pity for them, had no desire to pursue them and hoped they found their way to another place and a better life.

One day, she watched from her balcony as the water danced above, along with all the creatures below. The tide and waves had created a new flow in the ocean, and everything, including the creatures, swayed in unison with it now. As she watched, suddenly a bright light flashed before her, and she was unexpectedly transported to the same beautifully vivid place the mermaid princess had witnessed—where she found her husband waiting for her. Startled and shocked, she froze for just a moment and then quickly embraced him, sobbing uncontrollably.

"My love," she cried out as he held her in his powerful arms.

"Hello, my lovely queen," he said. "I am so happy to see your face, and I'm sorry I don't have much time. Our daughter has done it! She has not only defeated the darkness that tried to consume our kingdom but also released a whole new wave of light energy into the universe. We should be quite proud of her."

"I am." The queen paused. "I miss you, my love."

"I know, and I am very sorry I had to leave, but it was in divine order. I am always with you, and we will be together again. Be strong, and advise our daughter as she rules the light kingdom. She is powerful but will always need her mother's love. I have seen things you cannot even fathom— such impossible things. Our lives are connected, just as we believed, and this message must be spread. Teach creatures to love and be kind to themselves. Teach them that there will always be good and bad and that how they perceive these is what matters most. Teach them to look through eyes of love and to not judge or hate those who don't know how to do so. Teach them to do for others as they would do for themselves.

Show them what it means to be unconditional. And know that whenever you see a crashing wave or a light in the sky or shining stars, I am in all of those things. I am in all of life, and so are you. Live, my queen, and love fiercely. Though it feels long, time is fleeting and has no limits on the universe. Take care of yourself. Remember: darkness cannot exist without light, so if things go badly, do not fear—light is near." He looked deeply into her eyes. "Thank you for loving me with all you had. I will love you for eternity. Until we meet again."

He kissed her softly on the lips, and when she opened her eyes, he was gone and she was back on her balcony, staring out at the kingdom.

"I love you," she whispered, touching her lips. "Until we meet again."

\*\*\*

When the princess arrived in the kingdom, she was greeted by thousands of creatures, and her mother stood at the front of the crowd. They embraced for quite some time as the crowd cheered all around them.

"Mom, I—" the princess began.

"No need to explain, baby," the queen said. "Your father told me everything."

The princess, not surprised to hear this, hugged her mother harder.

"You are our rightful leader, my dear daughter. You will lead us all to love, and I am so very proud of you. And so is your father, who will be with us in spirit every step of the way." Her mother squeezed her tighter, and the crowd grew louder around them, cheering in celebration.

Suddenly, the princess remembered the gray-eyed shark was standing back, watching her exchange with her mother. She pulled out of her mother's arms excitedly.

"Mom, I'd like you to meet someone," she said as she grabbed the shark's hand gently and pulled him to her.

The gray-eyed shark bowed his head and reached out to kiss the queen's hand, but before he could, the queen put her arms around him and squeezed him tightly. "Welcome home, my son. We've heard how you battled the dark king along with my daughter. Thank you for all you did to help her return home to me. Thank you for loving her. Welcome home."

The princess's heart melted, and she joined the hug. The three of them embraced, and the entire crowd around them erupted in cheers. Everyone began to sing and dance, and a celebration of love's triumph began.